The Curse of Love Chronicles

BURNT IN BLOOD

By RJ Truman

ISBN-13: 978-1976075964

ISBN-10: 1976075963

Books by RJ Truman

THE WHITE LIGHT CHRONICLES SERIES:

Obsidian White-Shades of Violet

Vampire Cove-The Red Cliffs

Adrianna-Blue like My Heart

Lucy White-Indigo Skies

Rowena-Forever Green

Forgotten Families-A Yellow Ray of Hope

From Realms to Ruins-Orange Embers

COLLECTIONS OF SHORT STORIES

Tales of Tangled Thoughts

THE CURSE OF LOVE CHRONICLES

Burnt in Blood

Coming soon

Hunter's Moon

Contents

When I first saw you in the crowd,

Your face melted my heart.

And when I sensed you next to me,

I truly fell apart.

When I heard your voice,

A longing stirred in me.

I knew I had to have you then.

We were always meant to be.

PART ONE

Resurrection

Burnt In Blood

Awake but not aware

I can personally think of better ways to start the day other than waking up in a hospital bed. Especially if you have no recollection of how, or why you got there. All that Catherine knew was that she was attached to all these wires, and tubes. And her throat hurt like hell, due to the fact that a tube had just been pulled out of it. That however wasn't the reason why the name Catherine felt alien on her lips. It wasn't her name. This wasn't her body.

Waking up in a new body wasn't an unusual occurrence for, let's just call her Catherine for now. She had done it numerous times over the past a thousand years or so. It was just happening more and more regularly over the past few months. Which was frustrating to say the least. But it meant that she must be getting close to finally discovering the location of her own body. But I'll come to that later.

For now waking up from a coma did have its advantages. The main one being that you would normally have lots of people around you, filling you in on all the details of your life. Showing you pictures and asking if you remember certain things. And they would have no reason to suspect that your blank expression was because you had just jumped into the body. And had no idea whose body you were in.

As for her own body? Well that went the same way as all the others. In that it had burnt. She could remember that all too well. And it didn't hurt any less each time it happened. The first time was the worst, but each time after that the pain never lessened. She wasn't too concerned about the last body she had just left behind. That was gone. She needed to know about the body she was in now.

The details came in thick and fast. She found out that she had a husband. Brian. *Great, he looked lovely*. And he had a child that wasn't hers. *Which was also great*. Ok so maybe note the sarcasm here. The fact was that children only complicated things for her. Which is why she never had any. There was one in her first life, a boy. She knew that much. But couldn't recall much about him. Maybe he was just an outsider, like her. Cast out from the settlement because he was different? After that she was never in a body long enough for things like children to happen.

She also found out she was in an accident. Her car skidded on some ice. That was an important piece of information. It meant it was still winter. So she hadn't been in a coma for too long. She was hoping it was still the same year, and that a whole year or more hadn't passed. Which thankfully it had not. Back to the accident, there was a woman standing on the pavement, near to the wall she hit. The woman on the pavement with the two children was ok. She just missed them. There was quite often a woman and children involved in her multiple deaths, and/or rebirths. She would have to remember that. It had to mean something.

Sure the police would like to ask her a few routine questions, even though it was clearly an accident. And Catherine had come out the worst for it. Except that all of a sudden she was ok. She had woken up and miraculously healed. And there wasn't any signs of damage or injury to her. Apart from her memory. None of the Doctors, or nurses could explain this. And it's not like she could look up and say, "oh yeah that's because I'm an immortal, spirit of a witch. That is just hitching a ride in this body. Which would be dead if I wasn't in it."

Brian was on his way over to the bed. Thankfully she was well versed in dealing with the husband, in situations like this. She was also grateful that he had been advised to leave the child. A girl, outside as it could be too distressing for her if Catherine didn't recognise them. Her throat was all better now. But she was parched. So that would at least help her to sound a bit raspy.

Brian was all pleading big oval brown eyes. And floppy, greying, black hair. And he came armed with even more photo albums. And videos on his phone. This was all very wonderful. Except this wasn't his Catherine he was talking to. She was long gone. The woman in this body needed to get out of it fast and find herself.

She tried to let him down lightly. It wasn't his fault this had happened. It was just a case that Catherine's body was the only one available at the time. Catherine's ambulance was passing close by the scene of another crash. That was the one where her last body burnt. She had started to remember bits about that now. As that body was destroyed, beyond repair she had to find a new one. And when the ambulance passed by, It was just a case of doing a simple soul swapping spell. So poor Catherine's soul was in that body. Thankfully it wasn't in there too long before it was released, to go on and find peace. That was the other thing she didn't mention, as well as the ability to heal. She could do magic spells.

She instead went for the tactful approach of saying that, "Once I am out of hospital I hope you understand that I will need a few days in a hotel, or something. Just to give me time to think. And fully come to terms with everything that has happened. I will be ok, but I just need time. I've been through so much, it wouldn't be right on you and your daughter to make you go through it all with me. Please just let me do this. It will be better for both of us."

Brian like the countless others she had given this empty, meaningless speech to tried their best to understand. And would then dutifully make all the arrangements for her. Of course the option of staying with family, or close friends always came up. Which at first filled her with horror. Now she knew to say, "Oh no, I couldn't possibly put anyone out. It will only be a few days. I just need some time on my own to adjust and sort through all my memories." That line always seemed to work.

Alone at last

As soon as Brian left she locked the door of her drab B'N'B room. The walls were yellow, more from nicotine stains than anything else. The bedlinen looked older than she was. By this she was thinking of body, and spirit combined. It was floral in design but so faded now it was hard to make out the exact type of flower that patterned it. The curtains were thick and cream in colour. The carpet was brown and so was the furniture. This consisted of one single bed, a bedside table, and a small wardrobe.

She couldn't decide if Brian had chosen this place because:-

1. It was so depressing, he was sure she wouldn't want to stay there.

2. It was all he could afford.

OR 3. It was all this town, wherever it was had to offer.

Either way, she wasn't planning on staying long. Just long enough to get her head back in the game.

It was annoying that she wasn't able to jot anything down in a note pad. Or any other such device as people of this age seemed to use. She didn't see the point it's not like she could take it with her when she jumped bodies. So each time she had to go over a quick recap of all she knew. In some past lives she had time to go to a hypnotherapist, and counsellors. And spiritualists, and all manner of people in order to help her unlock her memories. Now she didn't have time for such luxuries. Not that they helped much anyway.

In all her years all she was able to remember was this. That she was, at one time a witch. That she was burnt alive. She assumed for some kind of witchy activity. And that there was a child. A boy. Who threw themselves on to the fire with her. And that's all she allowed herself to remember. That last memory was far too painful. More painful than being burnt alive countless times. Even if she wasn't certain the child was hers. The sound of his cries and the fact that he died with her, made the whole process of remembering too much to deal with.

In recent years, the only other thing that seemed to be a reoccurring event, was the presence of another woman. Always with children. Always watching her burn. That had to mean something. She just didn't know what but was almost certain that it was important. If only she could allow herself to remember. But the block in her mind and the walls she had built made it impossible to break through. She was at a dead end. She didn't even know her real name.

That she was sure above all else was the key to unlocking everything. If she knew who she was she might have a fighting chance of being able to look herself up online. An idea that seemed more insane to her than the fact she was a thousand year old witch, trapped in another woman's body. Until that body like all the others perished in flame.

If she found out her name she might be able to find out where she was burnt. And more importantly why. She could also hopefully find out the location of where she died. Once she knew that she could then try to resurrect her original body. And hopefully then find the peace she had been denied all these years. And why? What the was point in it all anyway?

For now though it was more death and banging her head against walls. Whoever Catherine was she wasn't going to be much help in the quest to find her original self. That said she would have to do for now. And while she was in this body, she thought it was about time she checked it out. She wanted to see exactly what it was she was working with.

There was a small mirror above the sink in the peach bathroom. Which if she didn't know better would have made her think she had gone back in time. A prospect that she didn't really want to consider. However if it was possible, she would have wanted to go back to the time when she was first burnt. Not to an era where peach bathroom suites were all the rage.

Looking at herself in the mirror she could see that she had shoulder length brown hair. It was greying at the roots. Hazel eyes. And a relatively good complexion. She had some faint lines around the eyes, and noticeable laughter lines. Nothing she couldn't live with temporarily. And after glancing down at the rest of her she could see she wasn't in bad shape. She was thin, if not slightly squidgy around the edges. Nothing a bit of gentle exercise couldn't fix. She wasn't hideous, which was always a positive. And given that her original body was more burnt than overcooked toast, she was in no condition to complain.

The mother of all calls

While perched on the bed pondering her next move, one of the worst things imaginable happened. Her phone rang. She gazed at it in horror. Brian had placed it beside the bed, maybe in hope that she would call him out of desperation and despair. And beg him to rescue her from this most disgusting of places. She told herself she would never be so needy as to run into the arms of a man. Well not a man like Brian anyway.

No matter how much she willed the phone to stop ringing, she knew the only way to deal with a ringing phone was to answer it. Even if it meant dealing with a call from Catherine's mother. Now she had dealt with all kinds of mother's in the past, from aloof, to overbearing. And had learnt that the best thing to do, was to always expect the unexpected. Mothers were a strange breed of human, as far as she was concerned. She had no recollection of her own. And after what became of the child, which was in her care in her original life, she had no plans to become one again.

The voice at the end of the phone was shrill, and over exasperated. "WHY DIDN'T YOU TELL ME YOU WERE OUT OF THE HOSPTIAL?" There followed a brief pause. More for dramatic effect, than to allow for an actual reply. "I stopped by the house to see that man child of a husband thing you married, and he told me. Honestly dear I don't know why you married him. And that thing he calls a child was there too. Now I know you were devastated when you found out you couldn't have children, and your relationship with that delightful Adrian, fell apart. But I'm sure there are better men out there with children than that drab Brian and his heathen spawn.

I know when your father abandoned us it left a mark on you. And you longed for someone safe and reliable. But that didn't mean you had to become safe and reliable too. I mean now you dye your lovely auburn hair brown, and wear those hideous floral sacks. Really dear, I preferred you when you went through that 'goth' phase. It was much more exciting."

In the time it took her to pause for breath, the new Catherine glanced at the black backpack Brian had placed on the floor near the door. No doubt then that it was stuffed to the brim with floral sacks. Like the one she wore when she left the hospital. Talking to this mother creature, had given her an interesting insight into the life of the woman whose body she now possessed. It also gave her hope. Catherine had a wild side caged up inside her. She could use this to escape the clutches of Brian, and carry on with her mission. She was suddenly made aware she had been silent for a bit too long, by the shrill cries of "hello," and "Are you still there?" coming through the phone.

It was time to face the mother and answer her back. She still wasn't sure what Catherine would say. But that didn't matter now, she was the new Catherine, one who had escaped the brink of death. She could say whatever the hell she wanted. "Yeah mother, I'm still here. And you know what. I've been doing some thinking. And you're right. Brian isn't the man for me. This isn't the life for me. I need a change. A fresh start. And a new look."

"Brilliant dear, that's amazing news. You and me. Shopping first thing tomorrow. And I'll take you for a haircut at that new trendy salon in town. Get your nails done. And then you can tell that Brian, and his little brute to shove it. And come live with me. Just until you're back on your feet. So to speak. How does that sound? I'll rescue you from that horrible old ladies prison he dumped you in. And you'll be back up and running in no time. See if we can't get you a nice young man. You know it's never too late. Just look at me and Michael."

She threw herself down on the bed in despair. The whole idea of shopping, and makeovers. Not to mention living with this woman and Michael. It wasn't part of the plan at all. Not that she had one right now. Besides she didn't need hairdressers to change her image she had magic. But somehow the idea of using that to change her look, and fleeing the scene didn't seem like an option. The next day's shopping expedition was unavoidable. If she was going to use and abuse this body, she would have to make a few sacrifices. And spending a day with Catherine's mother was one of them.

The mother of all days

The next day Catherine was woken up by the sound of high heels, teetering their way down the hallway. This was surely the sound of her impending doom. She turned over and hid her head under the pillow. Wishing she could just disappear. She hadn't had the best night's sleep either. The dreams, memories from her past lives were starting to flood through. They were never very helpful. All she needed to know was where her body was. Not how much of a great housewife she was in the 50's. Until she burnt the house down.

She could no longer avoid it. The mother was hammering on her bedroom door. So without further delay she rolled out of bed, and dutifully opened the door. Where she was greeted by a hug from a woman clad in black leather, and jeans. She had long blonde drip dyed hair. It was hot pink at the end, to match her lips, nails, and handbag. She looked like a nightmare version of some popular children's doll.

She hit Catherine with her itinerary for the day. Which she said at least a thousand times. The first part of the day was devoted to breakfast. Which the mother stated was "the most important meal of the day". Then it was off to the salon. Where she decided her Catherine needed a sleek bob, dyed dark purple. With magenta slices through it. This was closely followed by a trip to the nail technicians, to get sparkle dust put on her nails. Then to get some clothes to complete the look.

By the time they stopped for coffee, and cake, 'Catherine' didn't recognise herself. None of it mattered to her though. All she kept thinking was how much of a waste it was, and what would it all smell like when it went up in flames. She needed time to clear her head, as more memories flashed in and out of her mind. Memories of being burnt over and over again. But why? What did it all mean?

The mother was looking at her, it was a look that was halfway between intrigue and embarrassment. She was in the middle of discussing plans for a night out. To get Catherine back out there and showcase her new look. She had cleared it with Michael, and it was just down to fixing a date with Catherine.

Once the images subsided she looked the mother dead in the eyes and in pure disbelief uttered, "Get myself back out there, have you forgot that I still have a husband?" Not that this man or any other man mattered to her. She had never felt a strong attachment to any of the ones she ended up with. And not just because she wasn't with them long enough, she never had that physical attraction to any of them. She wasn't attracted to women either though.

The mother looked at her in disbelief, then laughed. "Oh I took care of him, I called him while you were getting your make-up done in the department store. Told him you weren't coming home, and to expect the divorce papers through the post." She smiled and crossed her arms, feeling all pleased with herself.

Catherine wasn't really mad at the mother, but she needed to get away from her. She wasn't lying when she said her head was pounding, and she needed to get some air. But when she found out that she couldn't escape to her B'n'b room, as Brian had only paid for one night, and most probably stopped her allowance, and credit cards. She knew she was fucked. Her mother delighted in telling her that Brain had at least had the balls to finally put his foot down. Whether or not he would follow through, she wasn't so sure.

It was then that she turned her mind to magic. She had stolen in the past. And moved items using her powers. Now she wanted to combine the two skills. The mother had tonnes of cash in her purse. All she needed to do was will it into her back pocket. After a few attempts, screwed up faces, and blank looks of concentration, she felt her back pocket of her super tight jeans expand. Without a second thought she stood up, and announced she needed fresh air.

There was a bus stop across the busy street, and she had sensed a bus was on its way. In her mind's eye she had already seen that the bus was heading to the City Centre. And that was the perfect place to escape to so she could plot her next move. She was safely seated on the bus before the mother had realised she was no longer in the street. The mother had been busy chatting to a young waiter, she was eager to know his opinions on her daughters 'hot' new look. When she glanced out to show him her daughter, he apparently hadn't noticed her, the mother shrieked in horror. Catherine was gone.

Next stop no Direction

By the time the bus pulled into the station Catherine was certain of one thing. She didn't have a clue what she was doing. She didn't know where to go. Or what to do next. After all her years of body jumping she should have been able to formulate a plan by now. She thought back to what she did in the past. Escaping one body, to end up in another. That was the basic gist of it. There wasn't much planning involved with that. It just kind of happened.

She did do research into witches, and places where their bodies were burnt. But as you can imagine there were endless places, up and down the country. And every time she went to visit one she would burn, and wake up in a new body. Then she would have to start all over again. The thoughts and memories would flood in. She would decide on a destination, and bam. Some awful accident would take place. She dreaded to think of how many bodies she had burnt her way through. Why what was it all for? Why did she keep coming back? She needed a body, her body. But what was next after that?

All she needed for now was a place to stay. Somewhere she would be safe. So she could plan her next move. This time she was determined she would make some real progress. And find out something new about herself. A key to unlocking the name of the place where she was first burnt to death. And the library was always a good place to look.

The next thing to do was to find it. Maps of the city were always helpful. And luckily for Catherine there was one at the bus station. She didn't have to bring attention to herself by asking for directions. She was sure by now the mother would be looking for her. She needed to work on her appearance. Make herself blend in more. But that wasn't something she could do out in the open. That would definitely draw unwanted attention to her, if her hair magically grew and changed colour. Or her outfit altered suddenly people would start to ask all kinds of questions. Ones she didn't want to, or know how to answer.

She could however make subtle changes. It had started to rain. So she could add a curl to her hair. And after hiding round a corner, she changed her high shoes for pumps. They were much more comfortable and practical. She had a long walk ahead of her. The library was on the over side of the city. And the best way to travel under the radar was to go on foot.

Buried in Books

When she arrived at the library she was soaked. She had also managed to add a few inches to her hair, and ditch the magenta streaks. It's amazing what she could do rushing through the smaller side streets and back alleys. In the warm air of the library, as her hair began to dry she lightened it a few shades. Dry hair was normally lighter than wet hair. So this little change wouldn't cause any unwanted attention.

She couldn't help but notice all the posters, and banners up in the entrance and inside the Library. There was an event going on at the castle in the centre of the city. Some kind of 'magical' witchy thing. This was sure to work in Catherine's favour, it meant there would be plenty of people around with a common interest. Although it almost seemed too perfect. Like things were finally starting to come together for her. It also meant that there were loads of books on witches, and magical history in the library. As much as that was a great thing. It meant more books. It also meant lots more reading to do.

Catherine was able to narrow the search by looking at books that concentrated on witch trials. Then weed out the ones that mentioned burning witches. And the places where the bodies were burnt. This still left her plenty of books to get through. And as she didn't have a library card, she had lots of reading to do, very quickly. It wasn't long before the library was due to close for the night. And she was keen to get to the magical fair at the castle.

Even with the ability to speed read the mountain of books just didn't seem to be going down. And what was more frustrating, was that they weren't giving her any new, or helpful information. They listed names of ancient sites, medieval monuments, and places thought to have 'magical' powers. They also named a few towns where witch trials took place. None of which were old enough for how long 'Catherine' had been around. She knew she predated townships. In her flashbacks she remembered living in a small straw hut like building. There were no bricks and mortar in sight.

With more books than she knew what to do with, Catherine was about to give up all hope. She was in over her head. Drowning in ink, and paper. Great she thought, *I've been burnt alive, several times, now I may as well be buried alive, under a pile of books!* In her mind she was frantically launching books out, like missiles all over the library. While in another daydream, they were raining down on her. All she knew in reality was it was time to call it a day.

All's fair in Magic and Mystery

Just when Catherine was about to give up, and leave, she overheard two people talking about the fair. Without wanting to seem too forward, she looked for an opening in the conversation. Causally she walked past the pair, and dropped the last one of her books on to the floor. Not very subtle, but it did the trick.

The man, tall, nondescript with short cropped brown hair, and a neatly trimmed beard bent down to pick up the book. The woman, who was younger than him, was slim with shoulder length blonde hair. She rolled her eyes, it was like women always threw themselves at Mr Hatfield. It must have been down to the size of his, let's go with intellect. Either way, he wasn't really her type.

He smiled when he saw the title of the book, 'The Trails, and Tribulations of Witches.' This was one of his specialist subjects. And one that as a teacher of history, to teenage, and younger students, was forced to study in his spare time. Abby was a former pupil of his, and shared his love of all things dark, and mystical. Her girlfriend of many years did not. So together with Mr Hatfield, she was giving a 'talk' at the fair later that evening. Abby couldn't get used to call him Stan, or Stanley. He was always going to be Mr Hatfield to her.

Stan passed the book back to Catherine, and his smile spread up to his eyes. "If its witches, and the paranormal that you're into. You really should head over to the castle. The fair will really be kicking off by now. Myself, and my colleague, Abigail, are giving a talk there later. You should stop by. I'm Stan by the way." He handed Catherine a crumpled up programme from his back pocket.

Catherine smiled back, took the programme, and awkwardly introduced herself. "Hi I'm Ca..." she paused. The last thing she wanted to do was give away her name. Especially as she was convinced by now, that the mother would have launched a full scale manhunt to look for her. That said she had started with Ca, she needed to follow it up with something. "Callie, I'm Callie, and I'm new here. So yeah I'll definitely check this out. Thanks. It's just my kind of thing as it happens." She could feel herself burning up, and dying again. This time of embarrassment.

Abby pulled on the sleeve of Mr Hatfield's burgundy sweater. "Well we really should get going, we don't want to be late. Plus we need to pick up Lettie, and Suzanne on the way."

Stan gave one last pleading smile to Callie, and said as he turned to leave. "So I'll hopefully catch you at the castle later?"

Catherine, or Callie as she had renamed herself, returned the last of the books. She knew she had to attend the fair. And not to see Stan, who was no doubt with either Lettie, Or Suzanne. Not that it bothered her in the slightest. He was pleasant enough. But not manly enough for her. He was too lean by far. This was however, the first time she had ever found herself really taking any notice in a man's overall appearance. She quickly pushed any thoughts of Stan out of her head. She had a mission to accomplish. One that had consumed all of her time over the years. And one she very much wanted to draw to a close.

Maybe, just maybe, the answers she was seeking were going to be there. I mean they hadn't appeared anywhere else. But something told her to remain optimistic. Things were coming together. And it was about time too. She didn't know how much more she could take.

If she was being punished for what she did in her first life, (not that she chose to be a witch) then she considered her sentence well, and truly served. With that in mind it was time to attempt to enjoy herself. If nothing else this 'magical' event, would just be a group of misguided fools. Wasting money on cheap tricks and false facts. But maybe she could pick up a broomstick, and a pointy hat. Just for laughs.

There were plenty of signs up in the street, and let's face it, a friggin castle is pretty hard to miss. Especially when its slap, bang, right in the middle of town. There was also a massive inflatable dragon 'flying' above it, Callie was sure she didn't see that before. But then again she wasn't really paying attention. She was more focused on getting to the library. All that provided her with was a crumpled up flyer, telling her about an event she would most probably have attended anyway. After all what was any mystical, magical event without a real witch?

Sure there were plenty of 'witches' there, as Callie had predicted. Selling spells, and potion mixes, and magic healing stones. Callie stopped by a few of the stalls just to amuse herself. She wanted to correct a certain love potion that she found, then decided if anyone was stupid enough to try that kind of spell, then they would have to deal with the repercussions. And the beard.

When it got dark and the music kicked in, and the lights and lanterns were all illuminated, Callie had to admit it was all pretty magical. And the smells of all the competing incenses', and essential oils were surely adding to the headiness of it all. There was an underlying smell of something else too. A certain something that people seemed to be smoking freely. A smell that couldn't be mistaken for anything else. And that wasn't even masked by all the other competing aromas. Not that Callie was one to judge, after all it had its medicinal qualities.

In the centre of the labyrinth of stalls, there was a stage. One where bands were alternated with people reciting poems, and giving talks. Callie thought that given the atmosphere that was building, and the revelry that was taking place, to give a talk late in the evening seemed detrimental to the vibe that was building. Surely it would kill the buzz, and the magic.

She was pleased to see Stan, Abby, and who she could assume were Lettie, and Suzanne, standing at the bar. Which was in a small marquee that was constructed close to the stage. She decided to make a beeline for them. After all if she had unfortunately missed their 'talk,' she could at least get a briefing on it.

Abby had her arm around one of the girls, and a pint of some pale yellow coloured liquid in her free hand. She was passionately going on about something, and from the looks on the others faces Callie wasn't sure they agreed. "No, no I'm gutted that they decided to cancel our slot. I knew we should have pushed for an earlier one. As once the music started up, I said it would be stupid to pause it for a talk on 'witch trials'. But what do I know?"

The girl she had her arm around smiled at her, then added "Well Abbs, there is always next year, and we all got to hear it. And me and my sis bloody loved it. Didn't we Lett? Even the millionth fucking time we heard the new 'tweaked' and perfected version. So why don't we all just say it's their bloody loss and get a few more drinks down us? And just fucking well enjoy ourselves? Hey babe what do you say? Yes? Say yes? Although if you say no. We all know what that means? Make up sex. Oh yeah. You know it…." She playfully kissed Abby on the cheek.

Trying desperately hard not to look awkward, Callie attempted to casually interject herself into the conversation. While realising that

30

she was really just a stranger to these people; apart from a brief exchange earlier that day. Where she also interrupted them in while they were in the middle of a private conversation. Callie turned to walk away, but at the same time willed Stan to make eye contact with her.

It worked. Seeing Callie for a second time, Stan felt like she was definitely someone he wanted to know more about. "Hey Callie, is it? Wait up come and join us. Or better still, I'm hungry. Are you hungry? There are some great places to eat round here. This place has a real festival vibe, don't you think?" Finally he paused for breath.

Callie smiled her most engaging smile. She could have just summoned up some magic, and found out if Stan had any useful information for her. But where was the fun in that? Besides she couldn't always use her magic to get her out of scrapes. Or to help out with boring tasks, like housework. Or to change her appearance. Okay so she relied on it a lot. But never to flat out extract information from people, she might be a witch, but she was also still a human. Just one with abilities.

Gazing at Stan, she wasn't attracted to him. Not anymore than she was to anyone. But she still had urges. Things she needed to get out of her system every now and again. She was alive, of sorts. And it was fun to try out other people's bodies. She had to get her kicks somehow. Aside from her endless searching for her original body, she didn't really have much else to keep her going. So having sex, while hitching a ride in someone else's body, was pretty much the only excitement she could have. And it was so much easier to get it now. It seemed a shame to pass up an opportunity. She didn't know how much longer she had in this body. So it was time to use and abuse it a little.

Fireworks and Flames

Callie and Stan arranged to meet up with the others at the big firework display at the end of the night. I mean what's more magical than watching fireworks? Especially once you're a little under the influence? However all Callie was under the influence of were some very basic human wants and desires. She put her arm around Stan, and pulled him close. He didn't seem to mind, and as he was a little unsteady on his feet, welcomed having a body to lean on.

Callie looked around for a quiet corner, and finally found it behind a now abandoned stall. Stan tried to play it coy. But he knew that Callie wasn't really after food, and if he was honest he wasn't hungry for food either. It was just a case of who was going to make the first move. And as Callie was sure she didn't have a minute to lose, she pulled Stan even closer to her. He swayed on his feet, and she used a little magic to steady him. She was pleased to feel that she wouldn't need to use magic to help out with the rest of it. Stan was able to do that all by himself.

Not wanting to be disturbed in a public place, and as she was technically still Catherine on the run from the mother. She did a simple cloaking spell to conceal them. Not that she was sure they would need very long. Stan was already pulling at her clothes. Looking for the quickest, easiest way in. Callie could just cheat at that too. Why mess with buttons, when you could just pop them open with your mind? A little magic, always added to the excitement.

It seemed like Stan was very already very excited. Not wanting to waste any time he grabbed hold of Callie. And while he could just about focus he gazed into her eyes. Then finally he closed them, and kissed her. It was brief. Then he turned her round. Bent her over and without falling over, easily found a way inside. It was like all of the passion, and intensity, had burnt the alcohol out of his system. He had a sudden sense of clarity. He knew what he wanted to do to Callie, and exactly how to do it.

As for Callie? It was fun in the way that she felt disconnected from it. Like she was watching two people enjoying each other. And more than that she could manipulate them to do exactly what she wanted. She could feel every touch on her skin. His lips on her neck. His hand on her waist. Holding her tightly, as he pushed himself against her. But it felt alien to her, like it wasn't really happening to her. She couldn't connect her soul to the body. She couldn't make herself feel anything for Stan. Or for any of the men that had come before him.

Finally it was all over. They got dressed, straightened themselves out and stepped back out into the crowd. It was all so clinical, and almost business like for Callie. Stan wanted to hold her hand. For him they had shared a moment. One he had enjoyed and hoped to enjoy again at some point very soon. He didn't know if he would see Callie again, after this night. But that didn't matter to him. All that mattered was enjoying the night as it happened.

For Callie she didn't feel any more for Stan than she did before. It wasn't any less either. It wasn't really anything. She wanted to talk to him, ask him about his hobbies, and find out if he really was an expert on all things witch related. But she quickly realised that she had ruined any chance of doing that tonight. From the way he pulled her to his side, and playfully grabbed her ass. She knew what he was getting at.

The fireworks started and a panic ignited in Callie. Given her track record, it probably wasn't a great idea for her to actively seek out danger. Especially not if fire was a big part of it. Sensing her tense at his side, Stan whispered reassurances in her ear. Thinking she was afraid of the loud noises, and the sudden bangs the fireworks were giving off.

He took her by the hand, and she wanted to run. But Stan had a tight grip. He wasn't going to give up on Callie. He was going to show her that while she was with him, she didn't need to be afraid. If only he understood, that there was nothing he could do. All his reassurances were useless against an ancient curse.

Feeling a change of heart she decided to go with the flow. She hadn't got the answers she needed in Catherine/Callie's body. Maybe the answer was locked away in someone else close by. This body had its uses. It brought her to where she was now. And she had a good feeling about it all of a sudden. She thought that a positive outlook would be the best way to move forward. And get her through whatever was coming next.

Well what came next was a loud bang from a massive firework. It made Callie jump and lose her balance. Not great considering she was standing next to a bonfire. Nothing like tempting fate. Now I'm not saying she deliberately jumped into the fire. However when Stan tried to grab her, she did push his hand away. I don't know if she was trying to stop Stan from possibly falling into the flames with her. Or if she had accepted the inevitable. Either way she was once again being burnt alive.

Who am I?

She didn't know who, or where she was when she opened her eyes. All she knew is that as her soul left Callie, it jumped into someone's body. She was just pleased it wasn't Stan's. She couldn't cope with being inside his head. Not after what had happened. What had happened? She could remember the past few days clear as ever. Shame she couldn't remember who she was.

"OH wow! You're actually awake! You've been in a daze these last few days. Ever since witnessing that awful accident. The train journey home with you was a nightmare. You were totally out of it. Didn't even know your own name! I didn't think you had that much to drink. Unless someone slipped you something in that last drink.

Anyway have you seen the papers? Apparently that woman has been identified. I have no clue how. Some runaway called Catherine. Going through some kind of midlife crisis no doubt. She just ditched her husband, and step kid. And ran off. What it doesn't say is that she fucked Stan! But who hasn't. I mean what a slut. I'm not saying that she deserved to burn. But still. Well I have to dash, I've got that thing with Stan today. I'm so excited about it."

"What thing?" She sat up in bed rubbing her eyes.

"For fuck sake Suz! How can you not remember this? It's like my life's friggin work. Me and Stan found that site, where that witch was burnt, years before burning witches was a big thing. And we are going to visit it today! She was the first witch to get burnt! No not ringing any bells?" Abby was furious now.

So she was Suzanne, and this was where she lived with Abby. She wondered if they had sex in the last few days. She doubted it, judging by the way Abby was acting. And the way she had been totally out of it. Which was a shame as she had never been with a woman before. And now that Abby was talking about important 'witchy' things, she didn't think she would get the chance.

Was this finally it? Had she somehow connected all the dots, and ended up exactly where she was meant to be? The trouble was Abby was leaving, and going with Stan. So she needed to find a way to go with them. This was going to prove interesting. But hey, if she had been acting out of character, it was also the perfect opportunity to invite herself along.

Throwing herself up, and out of the bed she announced, "I wanna come! I mean if this is important to you, then it's important to me. It's about time I started taking this whole thing more seriously. I'm just sorry I hadn't done it sooner." She added a pleading/sorry sort of a smile at the end.

Abby looked cross, let out a loud sigh, then hit the wall. "You know what Suz? Part of me wants to say no, fuck you. Part of me wants to actually fuck you. And the other part of me is thinking you know what fuck it why not? If you are really serious about this, and about me, then you're right you should be there."

With that Suzanne, (as she now was) decided that it would be a good time to get dressed. She glanced around the small, open planned apartment. It was all white walls with mismatched wooden furniture.

There was a navy blue throw over a worn looking cream sofa. The sheets on the bed, looked well past their best. That said she had slept in worse. She was looking for a wardrobe. She located the kitchen, which was up a few small steps, behind the bedroom/Livingroom. Then she clocked a clothes rail with a multi-coloured throw chucked over it. There was only one rail, this meant she had a 50/50 chance of picking out the right clothes. She tried hard to channel some of Suzanne's thoughts, or anything that would give her a hint, as to what to go for. When she got nothing, she had no choice but to go for the grabbing clothes at random approach.

When she was dressed in a pair of very tight jeans, and a slightly too short purple top. She didn't have to look at Abby, to realise that she had the wrong clothes. There was no time to change now though, they had to go.

Abby was going to say nothing. But she was seriously concerned about her girlfriend's general state of wellbeing. "Um Suz your clothes are on the rail by the bathroom, but hey it's cool. By all means wear mine. I guess we are in a rush. Your shoes are the black pumps over here by the door."

Driving to Destruction

When they were all safely piled into Stan's tiny Fiat, he pulled out his phone and double checked the route. He was tempted to ask a thousand questions about Suzanne. Like why she was there? And what was she doing in Abby's clothes? However when Abby shot him the "don't even" look, he thought better of it.

Feeling an awkward atmosphere building in the car, he turned the radio on. The volume was almost too loud, but he couldn't be dealing with Abby and Suz drama. He had enough going on in his head. Callie had burnt to death in front of him. That was hard enough to process. Not that he wanted to keep that image in his head. It was the fact she lied about her name and who she was. It was all very strange to him. He felt used, which was a feeling he wasn't familiar with. Usually it was the other way around.

The roads were relatively clear as the city gave way to green fields, and rolling countryside. The sun was shining, and it was a lovely day to be out on a drive. Even if the destination was the site of an ancient witches murder. And they were going just days after witnessing a freak accident at a magic fare. But for Stan and Abby, this was the dream day out. It was what all their hard work had been about. It was finally paying off.

As for the witch spirit that was hitching a ride in Suzanne's body? Her emotions were all over the place. She was hopeful, and fearful. This was the closest she had ever come to finding the possible location of her body. All she could hope at this point was that they all made it there, in one piece. And didn't all die in some awful road traffic accident. Trying to think happy thoughts, she looked up at the sun. A blazing ball of fire, in the bright blue sky. When that didn't help to lift her mood she closed her eyes. But that just brought all the horrific images of the past few years back into her mind's eye. Nothing could help her now.

Phoenix Woods Development

Stan and Abby both seemed surprised to see the large boards, placed by the roadside leading into the woods. They were from a building company advertising the new houses, that had just been built in what was now being called Phoenix Woods Estate. It was all part of Phoenix Woods new Development plans. Well at least it was now.

Not one to be put off Stan drove on into the site. Thankfully it was Sunday, and the site seemed to be deserted for the weekend. In the centre of a vast clearing a few large houses had been built. Abby looked at them in awe, these were exactly the kind of houses she would like to live in. All shiny and new, with plenty of space for all her books, and research materials.

Stan seemed less impressed. And Suzanne, as she now was, well she was a little bit put back by it all. If this really was the place where her body was burnt, how could she find it now? Underneath the foundations of these lovely new houses. Was she meant to dig up their perfect driveways? And hope to find the charred remains of some long dead witch, hiding just below the surface? She really wasn't feeling hopeful about this place at all.

The three of them stood on a large neatly trimmed patch of grass, next to a sign that read NO BALL GAMES TO BE PLAYED IN THIS AREA. They glanced around at the houses unsure of what to do next. Stan and Abby had fully expected to go on a magical tour through the woods. Not stumble on some luxury new housing development. This was not part of anyone's plan.

While Stan and Abby stood; pondering their next move, something caught Suzanne's eye. She saw a figure move in front of one of the houses. It was in the far left corner of the clearing, from where she stood. But she could make it out its form as clear as day. It was the shadow, or figure of a woman. She couldn't make out her features, or see if she or it had any. It was also apparent to her that neither, Stan or Abby could see her. They were looking around, with puzzled expressions on their faces.

Leaving them to their musing, Suzanne set off to check out the figure that only she could see. She was so focused on following it, that she didn't hear Abby or Stan calling out to her. It was like the world around her had melted away. All that existed was her, and the mysterious shadow figure. It was all she could see as she walked up to the red UPVc door. The door swung open, and Suzanne stepped inside.

The house was empty, as far as Suzanne could see. She looked all around for the figure. In the two spacious sitting rooms. The dining room, and the fully fitted kitchen. There was no sign of anyone. Anywhere. What she could smell though was gas. She was all too familiar with that smell. Sensing what was about to come next she turned, and ran to the front door. It slammed shut. And try as she might it wouldn't open.

The strong smell of gas filled the whole downstairs. Suzanne tried the windows, as well as the backdoor. They were all locked shut. There was no way out. She tried to call to Abby and Stan. She could see them outside. But it was almost like they couldn't see her. They were looking right at her. And doing nothing. *Why weren't they trying to help?*

This was it she told herself, it was another dead-end. She was right not to get her hopes up. And soon enough Suzanne's body would be burnt, like the rest of them. And she would wake up in another body. Damned to start the whole, pointless search again. Any second now something would ignite, and the whole house would go up in flames. Taking her with it.

True to form that's exactly what happened. Except the thing that ignited was the strange figure of the woman. It appeared in front of Suzanne, as she slumped down by the front door. Gasping for breath. Just as she thought she was going to suffocate to death, boom! The figure caught fire. Taking Suzanne, and the entire house with it.

Stan held Abby, as she screamed out in terror, and tried to run over to the house. She had seen Suzanne go inside it. And the next thing she saw it all went up in flames. Crying, and kicking and punching at Stan, she fought to get away from him. But he was stronger than he looked. Finally when he felt that she had exhausted all her strength, he let her go.

She fell onto her knees and screamed out "Suzannnnnne! Nooooooo." Before all words failed her completely.

Stan tried to comfort her. And in doing so missed what happened next. A woman. Naked, with long flame red hair, ran out of the flames. She was holding another body. That of Suzanne. She placed the semi-conscious, very confused Suzanne, on the end of the drive. Away from the Burning house, and ran off into the woods.

PART TWO

Reconnection

Arisen from the Ashes.

She ran, naked, and afraid deep into the woods. She had little to no idea what had just happened. Who she was. Where she was. Or why she was running. Finally she stopped by the side of a stream, and fell to her knees. She was panting, and trying to catch her breath. Feeling completely exhausted, she gave in, and laid down next to the stream. She felt safe in the forest. Hidden amongst the animals and trees. She felt like she was home.

She slept then, all be it briefly. For she had the most arousing of dreams. She dreamt she was in a cage. Still naked. With her hands bound, and tied up above her head. Her back burned, and stung as she had been beaten. Her body ached from standing for so long. A man was talking to her, speaking in a language she did not understand. He ran his hands up the inside of her thighs. And forced her legs apart. He was bigger, and stronger than her. Even with her powers, she couldn't seem to fight him off. It was almost like she didn't want to.

She could easily have healed herself. But it felt to her that in some twisted way, she enjoyed the feeling of pain. It made her feel alive. So too did the touch of his fingers. They were now inside places that had never been touched before. No one wanted to touch a witch. But he wasn't afraid of her. As he pulled on her hair, and forced himself inside her. She felt all of his power, his anger, and his rage. It was almost like he turned it into passion. And when he was done with her, he left her naked and tied up. Locked away in her cage. Inside his tent. Where he held her captive.

She woke up with a killer headache. The dream was intense. And gave her a lot of questions, none of which she could answer. She was under attack from a mass deluge of memories. Everything she had experienced, in all of the bodies she had burnt through, was coming back to haunt her. She knew she needed the memories. After all despite the difference in appearances, everything each new body went through happened to her. She was the one trapped inside them.

All she wanted to know was who was he? The man behind her. With the voice that made her whole body quiver and tingle. Even though she couldn't understand what he said, and she couldn't picture his face. He still held a power over her. He was the key to making her newly restored body feel truly alive. She had to find him. Every part of her was calling out to him. It was time to leave the safety of the forest. And seek sanctuary in him.

Power Trip

Looking down at her body one thing was sure, as hot as she was, she couldn't walk about in the new world totally naked. Sure it would draw a lot of attention to her. Maybe even draw him out of the shadows. But that wasn't a risk she was willing to take. She needed clothes. And as she could feel her powers surging through her, stronger than ever before. Making an outfit wasn't going to prove too hard a task. All she need was materials.

Not one to waste the gifts that nature had to offer, she was able to locate a fawn, and some rabbits. With a quick stun spell, they dropped dead. And with a click of her fingers they were skinned. She was able to make up a fire to cook the meat, and as for the skins? She turned the rabbits into a pair of cute pumps, with little bunny faces on the front. The fawn made some denim shorts, and a deer patterned top.

She decided to work on her appearance too. She wasn't sure if Stan, Abby, or even Suzanne had caught sight of her. Not that they could really report what they saw. What did they see? She didn't know. But knew that her look was a bit too distinctive. With her waist length, wavy red hair, and bright blue eyes. So after trying a few looks, she settled on a short blonde bob, and brown eyes. She only had the stream to see her reflection in. But from what she could make out. She was pleased with her look.

Now she had worked on her look she needed a plan. Her best course of action was to head back to the city. As a witch that drew her energy, and power from the world around her, she would have endless amounts of energy in a city. This thought made her smile, the fact she still had to get there however did not. She could use the lure of the energy to set her course. She would still have to walk it.

And walk it she did. She went back the way that Stan and the other's had travelled. And as she trekked down the long endless roads, she regretted her choice of footwear. As cute as they were, they weren't the most practical choice. There was no cushioned for her feet, against the endless pounding on the road. She spent a vast amount of time, thinking what shoes would have been a better choice. Finally deciding that nothing could save her feet. They were doomed.

After what felt like forever, and a bit longer, she saw a sign that made her want to weep. It gave her the distance, 3 miles until she got to her destination. She could do this she told herself. Only 3 more friggin' miles. It was nothing. She walked, ran, skipped, galloped, and even hopped some of it. To make it all that much more exciting. Anything to get her to the city.

It paid off. She was less than a mile away. She followed the river some of the way. She had spent so much time, thinking about her feet. And her head, that still hurt. She realised she still had no real plan. She had nowhere to stay. No family. No job. No birth certificate. Nothing. She didn't exist in this world. Sure she could magic up a bit of paperwork. But she would still need money to put a roof over her head. And there were only so many wallets she could take. She couldn't pick pocket enough for a deposit for rent.

Down and out by the Riverside

By the time nightfall came she was exhausted. And found herself to be in a nice quiet spot by the river. Something about the sound of running water soothed her. Not that she would get to rest for very long. A whole new kind of nightlife happened by this river. Women in little more than their underwear, seemed to pop up from out of bushes, and behind rocks. All waiting for the cars on the road nearby to stop, and offer them a ride, of sorts.

As desperate as she was for money, and she did feel for these woman. However, she couldn't see herself falling to those depths just yet. She was a resourceful woman, with powers. She was sure she could find a positive way to deal with the situation. Plenty of women, meant lots of men, all turning up loaded with cash. She felt a bit bad for the girls, but right now they weren't her problem. She needed to think about sorting herself out, before she could take on anyone else's problems.

Sitting up on the bench, trying to look causal, she cast an eye around for any unsuspecting victims. It was then that she felt a hand grab her on her right shoulder. He gripped her tightly, and pulled her closer to him. She could feel, and smell his warm breath as he spoke to her. As he did so he slipped his free hand down under her top. As if to "Test the merchandise", that was how he put it.

But this little witch was about to do a test all of her own. She tried to visualise where he hid his money. She could sense that he kept it in a wallet. But when he started to kiss her neck, and dig his fingers into her skin, she decided enough was enough. Money or not, he was getting a rock to the head. It was only a small one, but she sent it moving at such a speed that it knocked his head back. And caught his attention. He let go of her for long enough, that she was able to get away. While he stood around searching for the culprit that threw the stone.

She ran towards the road, when another hand grabbed her. This time by the arm. He was taller, and stronger than the last man, who was short, round, and smelt like stale whiskey and tobacco. This man was smartly dressed, in a dark, expensive looking suit. She was hopeful that he would actually get some money out of him. And he wasn't just after a free feel. Looking into this man's hazel eyes, she wondered if she would actually go through with it. Or just take his money and run?

As he held open the back door to his large black car, she found herself getting inside. When he stepped into the driver's seat he locked the door. Her heart was racing. She wasn't sure if it was fear or excitement. And she had no clue where he was taking her. But as she caught the sight of an abandoned warehouse, after they drove under a disused railway bridge she almost went into cardiac arrest.

He stopped the engine, and got out of the car. It would have been the perfect time to make a getaway. But she seemed to be stuck to the cream leather seats. As he opened the back door, and climbed in she realised something. Neither of them had spoken a word to each other. She was no expert on these things, but was she that they were meant to discuss the business at hand. Before going straight for it. What was he expecting from her? And how much was he offering? And how far was she willing to go?

None of these questions were answered as he unbuttoned his trousers, and pulled her the short distance across the seats towards him. She knew she could use her magic at any point. But at the same time her powers seemed to have abandoned her. Before she knew what was going on, he had her pinned down, face first onto the seat. Her legs apart, and her shorts down by her ankles. He might have looked like a gentleman in his suit, but there was nothing gentle about what he did next. And she couldn't help but feel his choice of hole, wasn't exactly what she was expecting. This was a first for her.

But not for him as he at least was enjoying himself. And had a few choice names for her too. "Filthy Bitch slut whore!" was a personal favourite of hers. She imagined all the ways she would get revenge on him. Scalping him felt like a good option, when he tugged at her hair so hard, she thought he would snap her neck.

He kept hold of her hair, as he eased his way out of her. Her whole body was shaking, and her mind turned to what was coming next. For he had a look in his hazel eyes, that told her he wasn't done with her yet. With one hand holding a firm grip on her hair, he used the other one to pull off her top. She was now totally naked and exposed to him. He pushed her head down, she tried to struggle. He put his left hand around her neck, pulling her the rest of the way down.

He left his hand in her hair, playing and pulling at it. Using it to move her head, as he moved inside her mouth. She could feel tears welling up in her eyes. As she had never felt this powerless. She had never know this kind of fear before. And even as she tried to fill her head, with images of her captor in his tent. She knew that even though he kept her tied up, like an animal. He was nothing compared to the creature she was with now.

Just when she felt like she couldn't take much more it was finally over. He pushed her away, and shoved a handful of notes into her mouth. She picked up her clothes, and with whatever she had left of her dignity she got out of the car. It wasn't an easy task, her whole body was weak. And she was still shaking. Beyond the warehouse she could see houses, and civilisation. She could feel the buzz, and rush of electricity fizzing through wires, and down cables. Signals, and invisible messages were flying around in the air.

She pulled as much power as she could, from this new world that was alive all around her. And slowly she could feel herself regaining her strength. The help she needed was all around her. She just had to train her body to harness it. To absorb it, and utilise it. This was what was going to help her become the formidable force, she told herself she could be.

With a wicked smile on her face she turned around to face the man in the suit. He was getting back into the driver's seat now. With just the thoughts in her head, she was able to whip his head back. With such force she almost broke his neck. And then as she healed herself, she transferred all her pain to him. She decided death would be too good for him. She wanted him to experience all the hurt, and discomfort he had caused her. She wanted to see how much he enjoyed that.

Aunt Vi's B'n'B

Looking at that money he gave her made her feel ill. It was barely enough to afford a night in a hovel, let alone any decent kind of establishment. Not that she was sure she deserved to stay anywhere decent, not after what she just did. She tried to tell herself it wasn't all her fault. But she did get into a car with a stranger.

Forcing the thoughts out of her head she walked the streets. After passing row, after row, of identical looking redbrick houses, she was certain she wasn't going to find a place to spend the remainder of the night. When she was about to give up hope, she saw the sign. I'm not talking subliminal messages here. I mean an actual physical sign. It read Aunt Vi's B'n'b.

The building stood on its own, and was larger than the other houses around it. It looked older too. It had a wall around it, that opened up to show a large spacious driveway. It looked a little outdated, from the flaking white paint on the outside of the windows. To the floral curtains, and net that hung up inside. But it looked warm, and homely. Which was something that she needed right now.

Walking up the gravel driveway, she was suddenly aware she was turning up, late at night. With no reservation, no bag, no ID. No anything, other than a handful of scrunched up notes. She was conscious that she wasn't going to make a great impression. But she didn't have the luxury of being able to change her circumstances just yet. And for the looks of the place, Aunt Vi was in no situation to turn down a paying customer.

Knocking on the white wooden door, she waited. She didn't realise she was holding her breath, until a woman answered her knock. "Just a minute, I'll be right with you. I just got to find that right damn key. Can't see a thing in this wretched light. I must get that light fixed. Now where is it? Wait a second I won't be a minute."

There was a loud jingling sound on the other side of the door. Synonymous with the noise of multiple keys clanging together on a keyring. Both women were getting impatient. Aunt Vi was swearing, and tutting on one side of the door. While on the outside the witch paced back and fourth. Now she could have used her magic to open the door. But she wasn't exactly thinking straight at the time.

Finally the well-worn door creaked open. Aunt Vi had her lilac flannel dressing gown wrapped tightly around her frail frame. Under which she wore a long rose pink nightdress. She had sheepskin slippers on her feet. Her hair, which was cut short, looked like grey candyfloss on top of her head. She had a suspicious, but not unfriendly looking face.

She was waiting for this young woman, who had woken her up to ask her something. But when she didn't speak Vi Broke the silence. "Yes dear? How can I help you?" As if it wasn't obvious what the girl in the ridiculous outfit wanted. She continued. "I take it you don't have a reservation? Well not to worry, we have plenty of rooms. And I take it you're in need of one? So come on in. I'll show you to one that I think will meet your budget. Now what did you say your name was?"

Slightly taken aback by the comment about her budget. She was in two minds to walk away. Then she remembered she had nowhere else to go. And this woman was taking her in, even if she was running a business. Vi could have easily turned her away. Then there was the other issue, she could hardly turn around and say, "Oh I'm sorry I can't remember my name." Not on top of everything else. She had to think of one. Quickly. All that was running through her head was what had happened in the car. Although she had got vengeance, of a sort. The ordeal itself still left a mark on her.

She was aware, as she was walking over the patterned tiled flooring, towards the staircase, that she hadn't answered the last question. What was her name? Haunted by the events in the car she found herself saying, "Car……a. Cara. My names er Cara."

Vi stopped on the landing of the second floor, and turned to walk down the hallway. Stopping again in front of a door number 4b, she got out a key. She didn't face Cara as she opened the door. Instead she simply said, "Well that's lovely dear. Here's your room for the night. Sleep in as late as you like. You look like you could use the rest. And we will sort out payment, and such in the morning. Now go on in, there's a small tub in the bathroom. If you fancy a soak in the morning." With that she stepped aside, and allowed Cara to enter the room.

Cara was too tired to answer. Exhaustion had suddenly rendered her speechless. She collapsed on the bed, and was asleep before she realised she had closed her eyes. As she slept her hair unravelled itself, and fell around her shoulders in soft auburn waves. She felt relieved both inside and out. It was great to finally be herself again.

Dream a Little Dream

She was warm and in a makeshift bed. Not in the cage. Her hands and feet were bound. She was alone. But not for long. She could hear talking in a language she didn't know. But the voice that did most of the taking was very familiar to her. It was deep, and commanding. Whoever this man was, he was important.

It went silent. She could hardly hear his footsteps on the soft grass. There was no flooring in the tent. That's where she was. She could see that now. It was strange that she was not in her cage. She waited with anticipation. Staying still, on her side. She was afraid to breathe. She could have freed herself. But she wanted to know what was going to happen to her, now she was in a bed. His bed.

She felt him pressing up against her cool soft skin, and welcomed the warmth of his toned body next to hers. His hands started around her waist. Then he slid one up to her neck, and one down between her legs. He kept a firm grip around her throat, as his fingers moved inside her. Then without warning, he pushed her over. On to her front.

Her hands were still bound. But he freed her feet. Holding her arms above her head, he used his free arm to pull her up onto her knees. As he did so he forced her legs apart. He was so strong, and powerful it was impossible to resist him. Not that she wanted to. She had never experienced men like this before. And certainly never like him.

When it was over he held her for a moment. Then let her go. He dragged her up by her hair. And while he still had a hold of it, he led her back to the cage. After he pulled open the door he threw her back inside. Before locking the door, and leaving her there.

Breakfast in Bed.

Cara woke up to find Vi standing over her bed. She would have been angry, if it wasn't for the fact that she was holding a tray loaded with food. It consisted of a full English breakfast, a pile of toast, and a large glass of orange juice. In all her lives, in all those years, she had never been treated like this. It felt like she was in heaven. Food heaven. I mean how can you not love having breakfast in bed?

Vi broke the increasingly awkward silence that was spilling out into the room. "I'm ever so sorry if I was a bit off with you last night. Not used to people turning up unannounced at whatever time it was. Never mind, we will put that behind us. And move on. Let's not pretend you have anywhere better to be. Or that I have anyone else to attend to. So in short dear, stay as long as you like. I could use the company. Now eat up my love. You could also do with a bit of meat on your bones." With that she placed the tray on Cara's lap and left the room.

Cara was in shock, she realised that her hair was now back to its original colour. As for her eyes, she had no clue what colour they were. Had Vi suspected magic was at play? Doubtful. Cara's second thought was, that Vi was so out of it the night before, she didn't take much notice in her appearance. Either way her food was calling out to her. And she had every intention of responding to it.

She cleared the first plate. Two sausages, a mountain of scrambled egg, four rashers of bacon, mushrooms, (not her favourite of things) beans, and finally two hash browns. All went down without a struggle. Then she tackled the toast. While sipping down the juice in between mouthfuls. By the end of it she was ready to take on the world. But she decided to have a bath first. Although she could clean herself with magic, having a long soak in a bath was much more therapeutic.

When she got out of bath and returned to the bedroom, she found new clothes on the bed. A clean pair of jeans, and a light blue long-sleeved t-shirt. There were no labels on the clothes, so they could have been stuff that was left behind. Not that it mattered. Cara had spent years in other people's bodies. So wearing potentially second hand clothes, was no worry at all.

Stay a little longer

While she was pondering her next move, there was a knock at the door. And before Cara could ask who it was, Vi was standing in the room. She was all happiness and smiles. Cara on the other hand was feeling rather confused. As if to answer to confused look on her face, Vi launched into action.

"I have been doing some thinking, and have come to the conclusion, that you need somewhere to stay on a permanent basis. But I can only assume you don't have the means to pay for long term accommodation. I don't wish to know your life story, where you come from. Or such. I just need to know that you are willing to work. As I happen to have a proposition for you. I need someone to help out around here. And you need a place to stay. So if you can cook, and clean. I can offer you a roof over your head. Meet me in the kitchen in five. And I'll see if you can make a decent breakfast."

She didn't stay for long enough to get a reply. And Cara was far too shocked to give one. She needed a place to stay. But she wasn't sure if Vi was being helpful. Or was a little crazy, and lonely, and trying to hold her hostage. Weighing up her options Cara really didn't have anything to lose. Or at the time anywhere else to go. If she was going to rebuild her life, she had to start somewhere. So why not kill a bit of time as some crazy old ladies live in slave?

After wandering around looking for the kitchen, Cara finally found it. Vi had laid out all of the items that she had put on Cara's plate. And then asked her to cook them. Which was an easy enough task. Then she asked Cara to clean the kitchen. She did all this while standing and watching. Not lifting a finger to help.

Over the course of the next few weeks, Cara got up at 6am. Went down to the kitchen, cooked the breakfasts. Then cleaned the kitchen. After this she cleaned the rooms. All this was easy to do with magic. Which she could use when Vi wasn't around to watch her. And made the whole situation much more bearable.

While she was there she tried to get a feel for Vi, to figure her out. Get her to open up about her life story. Sure Cara couldn't exactly share hers. But she wanted to know more about Vi. Who seemed to be friendly enough, towards the few people that came to stay. But she never really spoke to Cara.

This all changed when Cara got really fed-up one day, and started making changes to the rooms. Just subtle ones. Like making the dull walls more clean, and vibrant. And changing the curtains, from floral to plain. And getting rid of the net at the windows. She did all this while Vi popped out to do the banking.

You can imagine her confusion, when she returned to find the place looking fresher, and slightly more up to date. All Cara would say about the matter was, that she had her resources. And that every woman had their secrets.

Vi's Story

Vi poured her heart out to Cara, one Saturday morning when Cara had just finished cleaning up, after making the breakfasts. Cara was just about to leave the kitchen when Vi walked in. She perched herself up against the white cupboard door. Her ass resting on the black, fake granite work surface. She was wearing her favourite lilac sweater, and old lady trousers. Her face fixed somewhere between a smile, and confusion.

Her voice was firm, direct, and tinted with longing, and regret. "You're not the only woman with secrets you know? I have mine too. And while I don't share my business with just any old stranger, I think you've been here long enough now. To hear mine.

I met him when I was sixteen, we were young and in love. His family had money. Mine had me. And all I needed was him. It was all foolish young love. We got engaged. Then married when I was eighteen. He got us this house. With the plans to fill it with babies. Then one day, he got sick. And he died. And I was all on my own, with these walls to fill. And no money to pay the bills. He left me some, and with that I made this place into what it is today. I told myself I would never love again. And that at least with people around me I would never be lonely.

Somewhere down the line my parents had another child. They grew up, and had my nephew. And now he must be about your age. He's a lovely boy. Shame about his choice in women. Now Christmas is creeping up on us. And no doubts you have nowhere to go. So you'll have Christmas here with me. And my nephew, and so on." She unfolded her arms, pushed herself up to standing upright, and left the kitchen.

Cara's First Christmas

It seemed odd for a witch to celebrate Christmas. Yet here she was on Christmas day, in her Christmas jumper. With lights, and bells on. It was a Rudolph with a flashing nose, and bells on its antlers. An Aunt Vi special, as Cara called it. More to herself than anyone else. She still only had Vi. And the strange old lady, (who quite possibly wasn't as old as she seemed) was growing on her. All be it like moss, on the bark of a tree.

They cooked the dinner together, and laid out the table they even put out place names. It was all very formal. Cara couldn't help but wonder who all these people were. Brian, she hoped wasn't her old ex-husband from another body. Then there was Wendy, Phoebe, and Marcus. Lillian and Phil. And of course Cara, and Violet.

As it turned out Brian, was Vi's best friend. Wendy was an employee of his, that was all alone and had no family. She also had very pointed ears, and a small nose. Phoebe was the nephew's partner. Marcus being the nephew. And Lillian, and Phil were Vi's sister and brother in-law.

The dinner was delicious. Nothing to do with the added bit of magic, which Cara brought to the table. And the conversation was short, but civilised. It was clear from the looks between Vi, and Phoebe that there was something amiss between them. But they were grown up enough, not to air their differences at the table.

All in all Cara could have said her first Christmas was a real success. Vi secretly thought it was a shame that Marcus, and Cara never had a chance to talk. Phoebe didn't leave his side. It was like she was weary of Cara, and wise to Vi's plans to try and sabotage her relationship. But as they were all staying a few days, there was still the Boxing Day party to be had.

There was a scream, and something. Well someone went bump in the night. An ambulance was called. But nothing could be done. Violet was dead. The family all in shock left in the morning. It was clear that Violet's, adopted stray human pet couldn't stay on. Brian after taking pity on her. (Also because he owned a café himself, and knew from Vi what an excellent cook she was.) Had it mind to offer her employment. He didn't mind about her chequered past. Vi filled him in on how she came to her. As a woman of the night.

Life at Brian's

Cara was sat on Brian's brown leather sofa. She wasn't sure how long she had been staring at his freshly oiled oak floorboards. It was a stark contrast to where she had been staying. Everything here looked fresh and clean, and new. From the tab topped curtains, and fluffy cream rug. It was all pristine.

Brian handed her a drink in a mug that declared "life is better with unicorns." Apparently it was a gift from Vi. Cara could never imagine Violet buying such a thing. But it would seem that Vi was more of a dark horse, than a unicorn. What other hidden depths did that mysterious woman have? Now Cara would never know.

Finally Brian took the mug of cold tea away from her, and said something about showing her where she would be staying. The room was different in style to the soft earthy feel, of the brown and cream Livingroom. It was black and white. All the walls were white, except one. Which had some black and white floral patterned paper on it. The bedsheets were white. The duvet cover was black. And as for the curtains, one was white, the other was black. There was a clothes rail in the far corner of the room. It seemed only fitting that there wasn't a wardrobe. Cara only had a few items of clothes, all given to her by Violet.

Cara could see that Brian was talking to her. But none of what he was saying, was being processed in her brain. It was like the whole world was carrying on around her, and she could see it all. But she couldn't participate in anything that was happening. She could just watch it, with a blank expression on her face. She wasn't sure if it was shock, or grief that she was feeling. Either way she wanted to sleep.

When she woke up the following morning, she found she had company. A cat was curled up on the bed next to her. She couldn't recall anything being said about Brian having a pet. His house seemed to clean to house a pet. But none the less there was a large tabby cat, sleeping soundly on the bed with her.

After discovering the cat, she wasn't surprised to see Wendy in the kitchen, cooking breakfast. Her ears seemed more pointed than before, and her eyes more sharply angled. Her nose was thin, and perfectly straight. Unlike her hair, that was a mass of wild blonde curls. Much like Cara's, only hers were red.

Wendy let out a scream when she saw Cara. And Cara simply said "fuck" when she realised that she wasn't supporting her sleek blonde, bob with brown eyes. She was there in all her auburn glory. Staring at her reflection in the kitchen window. There wasn't time to magic herself back, to the way Wendy was used to seeing her. Not now, it was far too late for that.

Brian finally appeared, dressed in a blue hoody, and grey jogging bottoms. He ran his fingers through his short brown hair, and squinted his almond shaped greyish eyes, with a hint of yellow. He was looking at Cara. Trying to figure out if it really was her.

He spoke in a causal tone, that didn't really reflect the mood or atmosphere in the room. "Well it looks like it's a morning for revelations doesn't it? So while we are all here, allow me to introduce myself to you as the real me. I'm Brian, and I turn into a cat. And as I turn into a pussy it stands to reason that I like cock. Wendy over there is an elf. Not a house elf, or one from the woodland realm, just a common old regular elf. And as for Cara well, she could seem to be a master of disguise. She busting with power, and if my animal senses aren't mistaken I'm guessing she's a witch. And one in need of a cat. Which brings us full circle back to me."

After the air had cleared, and they all knew who, and what they were life at Brian's was a breeze. In the days leading up to New Year, when he was going to reopen his café, the three of them spent all their time drinking, and doing silly magic tricks. And living carefree. Cara felt like she had found a place where she belonged.

As for working in the café? Everything was easier with a witch around. She could cook, clean, and wash dishes all with the flick of her wrist. A mere click of her fingers, and bam! Any job that needed to be doing was done. Brian wished he had hired a witch years ago, instead of an elf. Who was useful enough. But not anywhere near as efficient. For work Cara kept the short blonde bob. She wasn't sure she was ready to be her real self with the rest of the world.

All up in Flames

It was a few days after Violet's funeral. And Brian decided he needed a night out on the town. He invited Cara, and Wendy along. He wanted them to see how his 'people' partied. To start with Cara was excited, expecting to meet more shape shifters. Or werecats. But when a group of well groomed, handsome men showed up at the house, she knew what Brain meant.

Wendy wasn't as shocked when she showed up, dressed in a short red dress. And very high red shoes. It seemed like she had a better idea as to what kind of night was in store. Cara quickly adjusted her outfit, from the long black velvet dress she was wearing, to a short back lace skirt. And corset style top. She still wanted a gothic style look. Just a little bit sexier.

The alcohol seemed to be flowing freely. And the conversation was colourful. There were a few remarks made about Wendy's wild hair. And some talk about having it 'sorted out'. Which although it upset her, she didn't dwell on it for too long. Instead she drowned out the comments with singing, and wine.

After they had drank Brian out of house, and home it was time to hit the town. There was one club in particular that they were heading too. Cara missed the name, but understood it had some reference to cats, or kittens, or something feline.

While in the club she lost sight of Brian, and his friends. Wendy said she didn't feel too good, and disappeared off to the ladies room. And Cara was left to dance, and drink by herself. Being in the club made her think briefly about Abby, and Suzanne. She was curious about what she would had done, had she had spent more time in Suzanne's body. This seemed like the perfect place to answer that question.

Before she had a chance to really look around and check anyone out, she smelt something. An all too familiar smell. It was the smell of burning. Soon screams, and panic broke out. The club was on fire. And an announcement was made that they all needed to get out. They were asked to do it in a calm manner, and not to be alarmed. The message wasn't really getting through. It was chaos.

As she ran out into the street, she ran straight into the arm of a tall man. He had short dark hair, and hazel eyes. He gazed at her for a second, before his shorter, black haired girlfriend interrupted them. She was hanging off his other arm. Barely able to stand, due to her high consumption of alcohol. And even higher heels.

She could however still speak, just about. "Hey bitch watch where you're going. And get off my man, unless you're one of those. If you're from that club, you're a disgusting freak of nature. And you deserve to burn!!" she put her hand to her mouth, as if she was going to throw up. Clearly embarrassed by her words, and actions the man carried on dragging her down the busy street.

Cara laughed to herself, she was a freak of nature. Just not the kind that the ignorant woman thought she was. She walked a few more steps, and tried not to laugh out loud, as she heard the crack of the woman's ankle breaking. And her screaming in pain. It was amazing what Cara could do, with just the power of her thoughts.

She couldn't locate Brian, Wendy, or the others amongst the swarm of bodies that flooded the street. Everyone was bumping into each other, rushing as fast as they could, to get away from the burning building. There was no use, she gave up looking and decided to head for home. If the others were safe, and had any sense, they would do the same.

She was still learning her way around her new home. And as she had never been to this particular club before. Or this side of the city, she was a little bit lost. She should have tried to do a homing spell, to locate Brian's house. But she was too full of alcohol to be thinking straight. So instead she wondered off in what she felt was the right direction.

Looking around she realised she had ended up on a street littered with drunk people, and takeaways. Had she have been hungry she could have feasted on fried chicken, pizza, Indian, or a whole host of other delights. As it was she didn't have much of an appetite. Not for food anyway.

It was his voice that she noticed first, his accent was different from the others he was with. His voice was louder, and more commanding. And yet his friends were still laughing at him, and making fun of him because of it. Then when she walked closer to the doorway of the takeaway he was in, she saw him. And it was like her entire soul was ablaze. Her whole body felt vibrant and alive for the first time.

She glanced up at the sign above the door, before she stepped inside. It read 'Flames Grill, and Pizza House'. She tried not to laugh at the irony of it all. If this was him. The one she had been dreaming about, she hadn't expected to be reunited in a takeaway. That said every part of her body, and soul was screaming out that he was the one. She had never felt like this about anyone else. In all her lives, and countless bodies over the years. This was it. This had to be him.

Will was busy laughing and joking with his mates. They ruffled his perfectly styled blond hair, and made comments about his dark blue eyes. That would make ladies weak at the knees. And all the while he felt something inside. It felt like his body was burning up. It wasn't a fever, or the alcohol. It was something else. He could sense someone was watching him. He could feel her eyes taking in every inch of his body.

Of all the women he had been with, and that was far too many to count. None had ever had this effect on him. He hadn't even cast his eyes on her. And yet he knew that he wanted her. He had to have her. Whenever Will wanted anyone, he got them. Without them putting up so much as a fight.

Stepping away from his friends he walked towards her. She wasn't exactly what he was expecting. Not that he knew what to expect. Something told him she was 'the one'. But it wasn't his eyes. Everything about her felt strange, yet familiar. He couldn't describe what he was feeling. There was a question about what she was 'the one' for? Regardless of how she looked, Will could still think of plenty of ways he could put her body to good use.

His mates were watching, they had seen Will in action many times before. But never like this. Normally he would talk to the woman in question. Say something, compliment her. Make her laugh. Anything. Not this time. He grabbed her by the wrist, spun her around. And marched her out of the door. They all stood, staring in shock. And this mystery woman, she didn't even seem to mind. There really wasn't anything Will couldn't do, when there were women involved that is.

No Time for Talking

Outside in the street, Cara was intoxicated by the power Will had over her. He made her feel weak, and lightheaded. In a way that she liked. She happily let herself fall into his body, as he held her close. With one of her arms pinned against her back. She didn't care, as her back was pressed up against him.

He waved down a taxi. And pushed her inside. Talking in a clear, calm voice, he gave the driver instructions on where to take them. It was to a hotel. An expensive one. And one Cara as sure as hell wasn't going to be paying for. Will's clothes looked well-tailored and he smelt divine. She was certain he didn't want for cash. Not in the way that she did.

When they arrived at the hotel, the lobby was deserted. The clean gleaming white floors were not kind to the souls of Cara's shoes. Will felt this as he had hold of her. He could feel her feet almost give way beneath her. Part of him found this amusing. But he didn't want her to see him laugh. This wasn't a time for fun and games. Not yet. Not until they were alone together. For now he needed to focus.

The woman on the reception desk stifled a yawn when she saw Will. She didn't look very favourably at his choice of guest. The blonde 'Goth' with the brown eyes, didn't look good enough for him. Her mind wandered off as he spoke to her. And she handed him a room key card, she imagined it was her going up to the room with him. As he walked away, she wished he was under the desk. Oh the things she could do with a man like him. As the doors closed on the lift she cast one more glance at his 'cheap' date for the night. Then went back to daydreaming about him.

Will had hold of her arm. He wanted to touch her in other places. He longed to rip the corset off of her. To grab hold of the body encased inside it. He just had to hold himself together, until they got to the room. He couldn't risk trying anything before then. Once he got started he lost all self-control. For now he was just about holding himself together. But inside there was a monster clawing its way out. He was an animal. A true sexual predator. This was his curse. When he locked eyes on his prey, they were powerless to resist. Just as he was powerless to stop himself.

Finally they were in the room alone, together. The walk from the lift down the corridor seemed to take forever. Both of them were eager, and full of anticipation as what was to come next. Now they were in the room, neither of them were safe. She was after all still a very powerful witch, even if she was under his spell. And once more all of her magic seemed to have abandoned her.

She felt his lips first, pressed hard up against hers. His hands tore open her corset. And his body pushed her down onto the clean, crisp white sheets on the bed. He used his knee to force her legs open, and she used her mind to open his jeans. She didn't want his hands to leave her body. They were running down her sides, until they found their way to her waist. Where they held on tight.

She could feel tingles of her magic inside her. It was like it seemed to kick in at opportune moments. Like when it came to removing his clothes. He didn't seem to mind, or notice that his fitted grey t-shirt was now on the floor. Exposing his toned, muscular body. And Cara, definitely didn't mind either. The rest of the time, she was more than happy to let him take control.

He briefly let go of her waist with one hand. Only so he could lift up her skirt. And pull her knickers to the side. She heard a slight ripping of fabric, and then she felt him. He kissed her as he pulled her closer. Digging his fingers into her sides, as he thrust himself harder into her.

She pulled away from his lips, and gasped for air. Her hands were lost in his hair. Her mind was full of flashing images. She was caught up between now, and then. When she was always tied up, and bound. Now her hands were free. She could run her nails down his back. Her lips could taste his skin, as she playfully nibbled his ear. Not that he seemed to like her new found freedom.

In response to her exploring ways to enjoy his body, he stopped briefly to turn her over. He dragged her down the bed. And bent her over it. So that he knees were now on the floor. As he held he pressed her face down into the bed, and with his other hand, held both her hands over her head. With one hand over the other, he had both her wrist pinned against the sheets.

It only seemed to take him seconds to reposition her. And it wasn't the last time he did it. He bent and twisted her body around, in ways she didn't even know she could bend. He held her by the throat, the wrist, the waist. And other parts of her body. He pulled her hair, and slapped her ass. And used every available hole she had. And never seemed to tire, or slow, or even pause for breath.

As the sun came up, and its rays seeped through the gaps in the curtains Will at last seemed to finally draw the activities of the night to a close. And Cara, was exhausted. Her body ached, and trembled. Partly with excitement, she had come so many times, she was surprised her whole body hadn't exploded with pleasure. And the rest was pure over exertion.

A little more conversation

Cara lay out, panting on the bed. She was trying to pull herself together. Will seemed fine, he was standing looking out of the window. He wasn't really taking in the view of the water. Just gazing into nothingness. Trying to get his head together. And make sense of what had happened that night. Sure he had enjoyed countless women before. Sometimes even more than one at a time. Yet none had left them feeling like she did. She made him feel strong, commanding, and completely out of control.

Then there were these crazy images in his mind. They were of him. And a woman. But she didn't look like the woman on the bed. She felt like her. Had the same power coursing through her. He could almost feel her magic pulsing through her veins. But her appearance was all wrong. She didn't have this fiery flame red hair. And cold, clear, blue eyes.

He needed answers. And now was a good a time as any to get them. Still looking out of the window, and not at her. Even though he could see the reflection of her naked body in the glass he asked everything he wanted, and needed to know. "Who are you? Where did you come from? Why do I dream of you? Yet not know you? It's like I've never met you before. And still I know, and want every inch of your body. I feel like you're mine. Like you belong to me. Like this curse I have when it comes to women, is a blessing when it comes to you." At last he turned to face her. It was her turn to deliver the answers.

The words that fell out of her lips sounded crazy even to her. But his face never once gave his thoughts or emotions away. If he thought she was crazy he never showed it. He just listened intently, hanging on to her every word.

Her voice was clear, and full of composure. Even if her body was a quivering wreck. She sat up as best she could, and even though he made her blush. She looked him in the eyes as she spoke. "I don't know who I am, in some sense. Only what I am. And that's only taken from bits that I remember from the past. It comes to me in dreams. And I've pieced them together, so they go like this.

I lived outside of a village, and one day it was invaded. A man, and his people came. They took me hostage. He held me captive. Yet I wasn't a slave, or afraid. He wanted something from me. I couldn't understand what. He took great pleasure in me, and my body. And I in him.

When at last it came that he couldn't get the answers from me, which he came for. I was taken from him. Tied up, and burnt. He threw himself into the fire to save me. And I believe we both perished.

Over the years that followed I have been through many bodies. Seeking out my own. Finally I found it. And then I found the one that was burnt with me. I believe that to be you." Her voice was slightly shaky at the end. As she was aware of how crazy the story sounded out loud.

Will didn't react, not outwardly. Inside his whole body, and mind were locked in conflict. What she was saying sounded right. But she still didn't fit the image in his mind. All his life he felt lost, like he was looking for someone. It felt like he had spent lifetime, after lifetime looking for the right woman. And now here she was. Finally. And she still didn't look right.

He had more questions. So revealed more of his story in order to get the answer he was seeking for. "I too, have lived many lives, all looking the same. I've met, and enjoyed women. But never been satisfied by them. So I have been unable to stay with them. Never held down a woman, or relationship for very long. And this cycle has carried on, relentlessly. I've been locked in it. Always unhappy, always looking. Hoping.

There was a woman, in this life. She was beautiful. Happy. Full of love, and vitality. Back home, all the men wanted her. And I was the one lucky enough to have her. I put a ring on her finger. An engagement one. She wanted to wait for the wedding night. I couldn't wait. My hunger, my curse. It took over. I had to have her. And in my rage one night I took her.

She was terrified. And I felt not ashamed as I should. But still I was vilified. Shown to be the monster that I truly am. I left my home town. And my name. I used my middle name. Moved here. Got a job, and made a life for myself.

Enjoyed all the women this city, and countless others have had to offer. And now here we are. I am here with you. And yet not with you. I feel like there is still something you're not telling me." He stood arms crossed, eyes fixed on her. Demanding yet more answers.

She knew exactly what he was getting at. She knew something else too. Some of his friends were making their way up to them in the lift. She wasn't sure how they found him. But she knew she couldn't stay. Without answering any more of his questions. She got off of the bed. Gathered up her clothes, and quickly got dressed. As best she could. With what was left of her clothes. She was also able to take something of his. Without him noticing. He was too busy watching her, impressed with how quickly she could move.

Without saying goodbye she walked out of the room. And in the corridor she changed her ripped up rags into a fitted black vest top, and black skinny jeans. As for her hair it turned black to suit her mood, and flowed down her back. Stopping at her waist. She made sure that Will's friends clocked her walking down the corridor as they walked up it. And she glanced back, making a point of looking at his door. So they could make no mistake as to where she came from.

Where there's a Will

Harry, and Jake practically pounded Will's door in. While he frantically dressed himself. When he checked himself over in the mirror, and was satisfied with how he looked. His hair was perfectly in place. And none of the marks, that the mystery witch woman had left on him were showing. He took a deep breath, and let them in.

They laughed about how he had two women in one night. And to start with Will was confused. Then he realised that Cara was a witch, and capable of lots of things. Changing her appearance at will seemed to be one of them. However even the description of her with dark hair, didn't seem right. He remembered a fiery redhead. Not a bright blonde, or mysterious black-haired beauty.

Will didn't bother to ask how they found him. He always had the same room. In the same hotel. In some ways he was a creature of habit. Just as his mates didn't ask how he came to have the second woman. With the wonders of the modern world, and all the apps around it was all just a case of a simple swipe or click. And when you looked like Will, his mates assumed he would be inundated with offers.

When it came to checking out, Will couldn't help but notice Jenny was still on reception. He had seen the way she looked at him, when he walked in with Cara. It was like he could read her mind. Jake and Harry were already half way across the lobby, when they stopped to notice Will chatting up the girl on the reception desk.

Jenny couldn't believe her luck, Mr Two ladies in one night (she had noticed the dark-haired woman leave with a smile on her face) was now finally noticing her. So when he asked "What time do you leave?

As I want to eat you out for breakfast. I mean take you out to eat breakfast?" She almost fainted. And was thrilled when Mike turned up to take over the morning shift.

On the way out Will couldn't help but grab her ass. He causally slipped a finger between her legs, and feeling around for a second he found the perfect spot. Jenny let out a playful giggle. And a gentle sigh as he pressed his finger into her a little bit harder. She didn't care if anyone saw her leave with him. She wanted the world to see.

Needless to say they didn't go for breakfast. Will hailed a taxi, and invited himself back to Jenny's place. She was relieved that her roommate was away on holiday with her boyfriend. Especially as Will kept up his end of the deal, and spent a rather sizeable amount of time with his head and tongue between her legs. Not that she was complaining one bit. She couldn't help but look down into his deep blue eyes, and think *fuck me how did I get to deserve this.*

When he left her she was lost for words. Staring at the ceiling in shock. She was completely out of breath. And exhausted. And not entirely sure what had happened to her. And the fact that when he was done, he just up and left. She didn't know if she was upset or relieved. Either way she was sure, that she would never meet another guy like him again. And was undecided as to whether she wanted to.

Cooking up a Storm

Cara left Will, feeling rather pleased with herself. But she also realised she was massively late for work. And still hadn't been back to the house. For all she knew her friends could be burnt to a crisp. She was in two minds what to do. And in the end decided to head straight for the café.

She was thrilled to see Brian and Wendy were both there, safe and sound. And rushed off their feet. They were confused at first when Cara walked in. But after she popped into the toilet for a quick change of her hair, and clothes. And walked out as the Cara they knew, and loved, it all made sense. And all was forgiven, as soon as she stepped into the kitchen, and her magic took over and did all the work.

It gave them all a chance for a quick catch up. And for Cara to fill them in on most of the details, of where she ended up the night before. And while Brian and Wendy, and the others were worried sick about Cara, they were pleased to know she was having fun. When she showed them Will's watch, that she had pocketed, Brian could only assume that it was the perfect payment for the night she had. Thinking to himself that old habits must die hard. After all Vi did say that Cara had come from the streets.

The lunchtime rush slowly drew to a close, and at three o'clock they called it a day. Cara was secretly hoping that Will would just happen, to walk past. Or pop in for a bite to eat, she had no idea he was eating out, elsewhere. While she slipped his watch onto her wrist, and held it close to her skin. If she really wanted to find him again, she could. But the next time she wanted him to find her.

The next few days passed by in a blur. With Cara constantly thinking about Will. He was thinking about Cara too. In a different way. He was still frustrated about why she felt the need to hide her true identity from him. And was sure at some point he would get to the bottom of it all. Until then, he was busy getting to the bottom of other things shall we say.

Just as she was giving up hope, of ever seeing him again she felt something. It was that familiar, burning, tingling sensation all over her body. And as Will walked down the street, with a group of his mates, he felt it too. As he got closer to the café the feeling for both of them intensified. Cara was thankfully all alone, closing up. It was Saturday, Brian had a date. Wendy had some elf business to attend to.

Hearing his voice as he got closer, Cara decided to causally step out for some air. And not so coolly, walked right into Will. Or maybe she planned it? Either way it worked, as it certainly got her noticed. By all the guys, not just Will. Who had to do a double take at first. She looked different again in her white work shirt, and black trousers.

The feeling that rushed through him were unmistakable. And he just couldn't help himself. He grabbed her by the arm, and marched her back into the café. She had a million questions she wanted to ask him. All different variations on "where the fuck have you been?" but she didn't get to ask them. Will had her perched down on top of one of the slightly cleaner tables, and was kissing her hard.

He stopped kissing her for long enough to whisper into her ear, "I want to see the real you." He closed his eyes, and ripped open her shirt. She did her usual trick of whipping off his jeans using magic. And when he opened his eye, she was dressed in a pencil skirt. And had a white shirt on, that was open enough to show hints of a red bra. Her hair was long, dark, and tied up into a high ponytail. And she was wearing glasses. When he looked around, he saw that they were now in an office. It wasn't exactly what he had in mind. But it was definitely a scenario he could work with.

He pulled her off of the desk, turned her round, pushed up her skirt. Then grabbed hold of her ponytail. This time she wasn't wearing any underwear other than the bra. Which he would remove later. Bending her over the desk, with one hand pulling hard on her hair. He fucked her quickly, and stopped suddenly. Turning her round, and placing both hands firmly on her shoulders, her forced her onto her knees. Then wrapping one hand around her ponytail, the other he used to once more rip open her shirt. He made full use of her mouth. Using his grip on her ponytail to work her head back and forth.

Still not content that he was making full use of his new surroundings, he dragged her, by the throat over to the photocopier. Once he had successfully liberated her from her bra, he finished up by bending her over the copier. With her breast pressed against the cold glass of the copier. She really had to get up onto tiptoes. Until she found the strength to magic up some higher heels on her shoes.

At last it was all over. Cara, was exhausted. And quickly the room faded back into the familiar old café that they were really in. Will didn't say a word, he picked up his clothes. Dressed, and left. He was still frustrated that he hadn't seen the real Cara. Sure the magic show she put on was impressive. But he wanted the real deal. After all he had waited long enough for it.

That said it didn't stop him from coming back for more. Every Saturday, for the next few months. Cara, was always more than happy to lock up on her own. And her and Will went through a number of scenarios. All the classics, like naughty schoolgirl meets dominant headmaster. To Drs and nurses. They even did vampires, and werewolves. And they were shipwrecked on a desert island, she was the siren, him the stranded sailor. You name it, they did it.

Then one weekend he didn't show. Or the week after that. And you get the picture. He had finally grown tired of her fun and games. He could have anyone he wanted. And the one woman he wanted, more than all the others, was in appearance, time after time, just like any pretty girl he could get.

Another Saturday Night Takeaway

Brian had invited Wendy over to cheer Cara up. He had also invited someone over to cheer himself up. He was getting seriously fed up, and drained by Cara moping around the house. After ordering a Chinese for them all, and eating very little of it, Brian and Tom retreated to the bedroom.

While Cara was pleased that Brian was enjoying himself. She, and Wendy were having decidedly less fun in the room below. And there was little, to nothing they could do to combat the overzealous noise pollution, which was seeping through the ceiling.

Finally Cara decided there was only so much she could take. And took it upon herself to declare that she and Wendy should head out. When Wendy tried to argue stating she wasn't dressed for the occasion, all Cara had to do was point out she was a witch. With a little bit of magic, she had transferred Wendy's fluffy onesie, into a tight fitting black top. And figure hugging jeans. She rounded off Wendy's ears. And even straightened her hair.

For herself she went for a long-sleeved, yet short dark purple dress. She was wearing purple pjs, and it was the best she could come up with. She gave herself long black hair, and smoky eyeshadow to set off her bright blue eyes. Wendy couldn't deny that Cara looked stunning. And Cara didn't say she had an ulterior motive.

She did still have Will's watch. So while she was dazzling Wendy, with her new look. She was also distracting her from the other spell she was casting. It was a simple locator spell that involved Will's watch, and a map. Once the spell had worked, Will's location was illuminated all be it briefly on the map. So Cara knew exactly where he was. And with her and Wendy, all dressed up, and ready to go in a matter of minutes, all she needed to do was summon a taxi.

Wendy should have realised what was going on, as soon as the taxi pulled up outside the hottest bar in town. However I wasn't until they were inside, and she spotted Will, surrounded by his usual crowd of loyal followers that reality hit. All this was just a ploy, so that Cara could track down Will. If it wasn't for the fact that some of his friends were, as Wendy would say "knicker droppingly beautiful." Which I guess works on different levels.

Will was at the bar, with his arm around a tall blonde woman. She was wearing bright red lipstick, which Cara noticed matched her nails, shoes, and bag. It also matched the stain on Will's neck. And when Cara looked again, she could clearly also see teeth marks on Will's skin. She was pleased that his skin was punctured, although she had never encountered vampires. In a world as it was, with witches, werecats and elves, Cara didn't want to rule anything out.

Looking cute, and coy, but feeling suddenly empowered and sexy. Wendy broke through the centre of the group. And pushed her way to the bar. Cara inwardly applauded Wendy, for doing what she didn't have the balls to do herself. Within seconds, Wendy caught the eye of Kane. He had golden brown hair, and hazel eyes, that had a wicked/cheeky glint in them. And they lit up when they saw Wendy, who introduced herself as Gwendolyn. Which made Cara ask herself why go for Wendy? When Gwen would be a much closer alternative?

Will could sense Cara behind him, and completely ignored her. He even went as far as to welcome Gwen to the group. Introducing her to all his friends. Including Skarla the blonde, whose ass he was

86

squeezing a little too tight. When Skarla tried to playfully push it away, he only squeezed harder.

Finally deciding she had enough of watching from the side lines, Cara nestled in beside Skarla, and some random at the bar. She wanted to play Will at his own game. So she placed her hand gently on the base of Skarla's back. Skarla blushed as Cara sent a rush of power through her. Not wanting to be out done, Will slipped his hand up the inside of Skarla's thigh. Taking this as an invitation to join him in a silent combat. Cara did the same on the other side. This was war. And the battlefield was Skarla's body.

Skarla didn't know how to react to the fact that two fingers, from two different people were inside her. They both seemed to know what they were doing. And the fact that they were locked into some kind of conflict, only heightened the experience for her. Occasionally other fingers would make their way in. One even made its way into a different hole altogether. It was like neither Will nor Cara wanted to be out done. And they had forgotten what they were fighting about in the first instance. Which was the fact the Cara was annoyed the Will was continuing to ignore her. And he was annoyed that she had turned up in yet another disguise.

The whole thing was turning all three of them on. And when Will and Cara locked eyes on each other, the energy that surged through them both passed through Skarla. Who was finding it hard enough to contain herself as it was. Finally overcome with power, feelings, and emotions, Skarla passed out. Will propped her up against the bar, and both he, and Cara finally left the poor woman alone.

Will was never a great one at self-control, he wrapped his hand around the back of Cara's head. She was expecting him to kiss her.

Not to push a finger into her mouth. Especially not one that tasted of Skarla. The others in the group may not have noticed what Will, and Cara were doing to Skarla. But they couldn't help but not notice, Cara seductively suck Will's finger. Jai and Crystal were the first to notice, and quickly, with the aid of elbows in the ribs, throat clearing and finger pointing notified the others.

Aware that people were watching, Cara cast a concealing spell over them. One that meant to the casual observer they were merely engaged in polite conversation. There was however nothing polite about the conversation that was unfolding. Will was still feeling increasing frustrated about Cara, and her ever changing appearance.

"It fucks me off to see you like this, yeah you look hot. But so do countless other women in this room. But none of them make me feel the way you do. Like my whole body is burning with desire. And I just have to have you. But I've had enough off all this. All these fun, and games have to stop. I want you! The real you. I want to know what your body feels, and taste like. I want all of you?!" Will spoke these words as he held Cara tight. One hand entangled in her hair. One had a firm grip on her ass.

Cara paused, there were a million and things she wanted to do, at that exact moment in time. And none of them involved showing her true form. She tried to argue with Will, and use the normal response of "But this is who I am." He wasn't buying it.

The Big Reveal

Will tried all sorts of things, from flattery, to flat out anger. Finally seeing that she wasn't going to win. Cara let down her guard. She didn't want to admit that it did hurt her a bit, to constantly keep changing her guise. And she was tired of fighting against her true self. She had waited countless years to get her own body back. Now she was hiding it away, and why? Was she worried of what the world would think of her? Or what Will would think of her?

She told herself that long ago, she met this man. And he wanted her for the way she was. This wild woman, with fiery craze flame red hair. And ice blue eyes. If that's what he's been hunting for, over all of these years, then there was no more time to waste. He was going to get it.

When Cara dropped the veil that she put over herself and Will, she was not only a bright haired beauty. She was in her nightclothes. He wanted all of her, with nothing to hide and he got it. And not just he was surprised by what he saw. His mates couldn't believe it either.

Jai looked at this wild woman, open mounted and asked "Will, mate how the fuck do you do it. I mean one second it's that blonde thing, draped over your arm. Then that other blonde. Now you got this bitch out of her bed! That's some serious skills you got there. She aint even dressed! Hi by the way. I'm Jai, and you are?" He directed the question straight at her.

But what could she say? She didn't know her name. Even if she could remember a name she had once, it was gone. Long forgotten, along with the life she used to have. Now she was born again, she could be named something different. If she was even named before. Flashes of her life flicked through her mind. Adding to the blank, dazed expression on her face.

It was Will that answered. "Autumn Ruby Iris. Well at least that was the name she had on her profile. And as you can see she was in such a rush to see me, she forgot to get dressed. So I think it's only gentlemanly of me to take her home. Wouldn't you all agree?" He didn't wait for a reply, he slipped his arm around Autumn's waist, and whisked her out of the bar.

Once outside she could feel an anger building up inside her. The windows on the bar started to vibrate, and the street lights all around started to flicker. "You could have picked a better name, one that didn't make me sound like a cheap whore! I know you're used to picking up women, left right and centre. But we both know I'm more than that. And how dare you fucking name me!"

She raised her hand to strike Will on the face. He grabbed her wrist. As much as she tried to fight it. To fight him she couldn't. He let go of her wrist, as it fell to her side he pulled her close. She didn't try to fight him off as his lips pressed into hers. A surge rushed through them both. It blew the windows out of the bar. The lights all around them flickered and exploded, and all the car alarms in the area went off.

It only took a quick flick of her wrist to put it all right. It was like the whole scene had been played back on rewind. The glass rose up from the floor. And settled back into place in the window frames. All the lights came back on, and a silence descended all around. Will was left speechless. Without warning he swept Autumn off her feet. And carried her to the nearest taxi.

The Elf in the Room

After Cara, or Autumn as she was now apparently called left with Will, Wendy was left without her witch friend. She was pleased to see that the magic seemed to hold. Even without Autumn being present. As things with her and Kane were starting to get interesting.

She couldn't find it in herself to turn down his invite to leave. And within minutes the two of them were kissing in the back of a taxi. They went back to Kane's. The moment they were in through the front door, Kane had Wendy pinned against the wall.

They took it to the bedroom after that, and while Kane was no Will in the bedroom, Wendy didn't mind. She was just so thrilled to be with someone other than another elf. They were all too slow, and sensual for her liking. Elves normally loved romance, and ambience. Kane was human, and more about raw, urgent human wants, and desires. This was much more to Wendy's taste.

The next morning when Kane brought the coffees in, he was shocked. Wendy looked different. He knew he had been drinking the night before. But he wasn't that drunk. The woman in his bed had crazy curly hair, a prefect slim little nose. And pointed ears. She was like something from one of his favourite movies, or video games.

Wendy could see the confused look on his face, and knew exactly what that meant. The spell was broken, and he had seen her for the freak she really was. She hid herself back under the sheets. Too ashamed to face Kane, looking like she did. How could he want her now?

In truth Kane had a thing for elves, and fairy women. The ones he had seen before weren't real. They were only on a screen, big or small. Now he couldn't believe what he was seeing. As it was like he had a real life elf in his room. He put the drinks down on the only space he could find on his over filled shelf. And walked over to the bed.

Slowly he pulled the sheets off of Wendy, and she looked around his room. All the walls were covered in posters. They were from scenes or of characters from his favourite films, and games. And there shelves everywhere, filled with everything from games to action figures. She hadn't noticed it before. Her eyes were locked on Kane.

Still not sure if he was dreaming Kane leant forward, and kissed Wendy. She was startled. But didn't pull away. She could sense this was him saying he was accepting her. All of her in her strange new form. She was very accepting of him too. So much so, that they spent the next day getting to know all the differences, between elf and human bodies.

PART THREE

Revelations

Curiosity and the Cat

Suddenly Brian found himself spending lots of time alone. Autumn as she was now called was spending all her free time with Will. And Wendy was practically living with Kane. He was obsessed with taking her to comic book conventions, were everyone was fascinated by just how realistic her makeup and prosthetics were.

So all alone again, Brian took to looking up random crap online. He was curious to know more about Will, and Autumn. They were like a celebrity couple, amongst the local Parahuman community. Everyone wanted a piece of the amazing immortal lovers. And this was part of the reason they took to hiding out at Will's place. He wasn't into the Parahuman scene. It was all too much for him, it was one thing to be dating a witch, it was another to socialise with other witches, and elves and fairy folk.

After hours of research Brian wasn't coming up with much. Just ancient legends of a beautiful witch, and her handsome warrior lover. And how they were burned together, and bound together forever. All stuff he already knew. Will apparently had several children in his past life, something he neglected to mention. Not that it mattered now, Brian could only assume they were long dead by now anyway. But was interested to know if any of them lived to have families of their own. Not that any of that was documented anywhere. It was all the myths, and legends. Very little real fact. It all seemed very mystical, and romantic. But he had heard Cara, now Autumn screaming out in pain in the night. Reliving those traumatic events, over and over again. Even the meetings with Will, didn't strike him as terribly romantic.

It was just as he was about to give up that an article did grab him. It was about a curse, and a blood stone. And stated that Will's wife, and mother of his children was the one that cursed Will and Autumn. She as you could imagine, didn't take too kindly to her husband, throwing himself into a fire. All to save some witch whore. And so as they burnt, and their blood flowed into a pool, she cursed the congealed blood. And them with it.

Brian was half asleep, by the time he finished the article. But came to the conclusion, to lift the curse they had to destroy the stone. So despite the fact that against all the odds they had found each other, they were still doomed. As in the next life they would be destined to begin the search for each other all over again.

He made a mental note to tell Autumn this, the next time she was in work. She still worked for him most days, and apparently still lived in his house. After all what was a witch without her cat? Doomed in this case it would seem.

Blood stones, and Diamonds

The next time Autumn showed up at the café she was met by Wendy, who had a rather large rock on her finger. Wendy was over the moon. And Autumn was thrilled for her. Brain just held on to the information about the blood stone, until the end of the shift. He was sure that Will the wonderful would show up. And rather than go over it all twice, it made sense to tell everyone together.

Right on cue as soon as he flipped the 'closed' sign over. Will stuck his foot through the door. He was followed by his second shadow, Kane. Just as Will was about to draw Autumn away, Brian made his move. Declaring that he too had some important news to announce. When he had their undivided attention he began.

Clearing his throat he loudly proclaimed "It is wonderful news about Kane, and Wendy. But let's now turn our thoughts to the other happy couple in the room. Our very own, infamous immortal lovers. Or Will, and Autumn as they call themselves in this life.

They too have their own stone. A blood stone. It seems that Will's long estranged wife, in his first life cursed the two of you. She wasn't all too happy with William's behaviour. What with him choosing the witch over her, and the children.

And so when you burnt on the stake, and your blood flowed together. It formed a kind of stone. She took this, and cursed you both. So that you would rise again, and again from the ashes. Always looking for the one that you lost. Never to rest, even if you were to find each other. For as long as the stone exists you will never rest." He paused, for dramatic effect.

97

Silence filled the room. No one spoke, or knew what to say. Will paced back and forth. Autumn gazed at the wall. If she knew more about the stone, she could do a spell to locate it. Then it hit her. Just as she was about to talk Will beat her to it.

He hit his fist down onto one on the empty tables. "Damn it Brian, and what use is it telling us this now. Half of this we know. The other half is useless. What does this stone even look like? How do we find it? Is it even real? For Christ sake the internet is full of shit about me, and Autumn, and our beautiful moving romance. If I believed half the stuff I read, I would think it was the most epic fucking love story ever.

But on the flip side is it even love? Or just some fucking curse, that we are forced to play out over, and over again? Are we really going to live happily ever friggin after? Or are we just thrilled not to be writhing in agony, being burnt over and over again, for all eternity?

Do you know what it's like to meet someone, and not be able to love them fully? As you are haunted by the face of some witch bitch, burning over and over again? Now you tell me there might be away to end all of this. Or is it just a fool's hope?" He turned his gaze, eyes blazing straight at Brian.

It was Kane's turn to speech next. He cut in before Autumn had a chance. She was seething from Will's outburst. Witch bitch indeed. She would make him pay for that one. Show him who the real bitch was, oh she could make him beg for mercy, just as much as he could her.

Kane spoke loudly, above the tension in the room. "There is a convention coming up in the capital. One all about mythical, magical things. Stones and such. It might be worth checking it out. I'm not saying that the stone will be there. But there might be someone there that could tell us more about it. Or that would know someone, or be able to point us in the right direction. I was thinking of taking Wend this weekend, as I'm sure that you can get tickets on the door, on the day. So what do you say we all go on a road trip?" He tried to sound upbeat and hopeful.

Finally Autumn got her chance to speak. "I for one think that is a great idea Kane. And let us not overlook the fact that this witch bitch, can do magic. And if the stone is there, I can do a spell to try and find it. Before you all doubt me." She turned to stare at Will. "The fact is that this so called stone is made from the blood of me, and Will. So not only is it ours, it's from us. So in order to find it I have everything I need. Which is me and Will.

To do a locator spell on someone, you need something of theirs. To locate an object, you need the person the object belongs to. In this case if me and Will are both there together, the spell will be easy. And powerful too."

That was it then. Settled. All of them would be off. That weekend. To the capital. To hopefully find a stone that would end the curse. Neither Will, nor Autumn really knew how they felt about that. This curse was all they had, it kept them alive for all these years. If they broke that what would they have left? Would they even have, or want each other? There wasn't any way of answering these questions.

The only thing for sure was that they were going for it. They were going to look for this so called blood stone. Everything else would have to wait for after. All their lives had been cast into uncertainty. And that's what made it all so nerve-wracking and exciting.

Set in Stone

They got together every day leading up to the convention. The meeting place was always at Brian's. And he always made sure he had plenty of food and drinks, to keep everyone's minds fed and hydrated. He had the art of entertaining guests perfected, right down to what scented candles to burn, and music to play to set the right atmosphere. Nothing was left to chance.

On the first meeting everyone was tense, and nervous. They had a few days to sort everything from train times, and accommodation. To how to locate, and acquire the actual stone. Should it be there that is. But they instead took to pacing, staring at the walls and drumming their fingers. No one knew how to approach the subject.

That was until Brian broke the silence with a loud sigh, before launching into a plan of attack. "Well I for one have an idea, the first thing we need to do is think of train times, Wendy you look them up. It will take us a few hours to get there, and we need to take getting through crowds and such into consideration. Then once we are there, we split into groups, or couples in this case. I will go alone, a cat needs no company. We will ask around for information about the stone. And Autumn, you can try and do your magic thing, to see if it's there. I guess you can magic it away, if it is, and then we all take off." He looked at the others, hoping for some useful input or feedback.

Autumn stopped gazing into space to say, "Yeah that sounds great to me. If it's there I'll find it. Now can we eat? I'm starving."

The next few meetings covered, and perfected all the points of the plan. So they knew exactly what time they had to be at the station.

How they would get across the capital. Autumn knew the spells she would use. And they had a hotel booked as a rendezvous point, and because they all fancied a mini break in the capital.

Another important point raised was what they would wear. Kane, and Wendy wanted to go as elves. Well for Wendy that meant going as herself, but Kane wanted to 'elf up' as he put it. Autumn thought it could be fun to go as a witch, complete with pointed hat, and broomstick. Brian decided he would go as a witches' cat. Will was still unsure if he wanted to go at all. And was just going as himself.

While all of the finer points of the plan came together, no one discussed what would happen after. Or if they didn't find the stone. Even in private Autumn and Will didn't talk about the stone, or the curse. It was a shadow that was hanging over them. But one they were both happy to ignore. Everyone else was seemingly excited about the possibility of finding this magical stone. And they were simply going with the flow.

Any initial feelings they had about ending the curse weren't discussed. They pushed all thoughts aside. All they had known up until they were reunited were their thoughts, feelings, urges, and desires. They never thought of the future. And now they were together they didn't know what to think. All they knew was that nothing was set in stone. Even this curse. But in order to not think about it, they had to keep busy. And at that time that meant planning with the others. So that's what they did.

Stone cold silence

When the day finally came around, and they all met at the station. In their costumes, cat ears, brooms and all, no one said a word. The only one technically not in a costume was Will. But he was going as himself anyway, and didn't require flowing elven robes, or a pointed witches hat for that. The costume for a slightly damaged, immortal sex god, was jeans, and on this occasion a white t-shirt.

The atmosphere between them all was tense, at best. No one wanted to antagonise Will, or upset Autumn. Whose hair was a particularly vivid shade of red. It actually looked like it was made up of moving flames, flickering, burning and interchanging in colour. It was both mesmerising, and concerning to watch. As the others were worried she would burst into flames, or cause a mass fire at any moment. Things between her and Will seemed strained, as she was growing increasingly frustrated by the lack of communication between the two of them. Will wasn't really one for words.

So Brian sat, gazing out of the window. Enjoying the ever changing scenery, while sucking loudly on a fruit sweet. It was difficult to eat hard boiled sweets, while his mouth was somewhere between cat, and human. Plus he couldn't stand the silence. So decided any noise, was better than none. Regardless of how irritating it was.

Autumn had even pushed the thoughts of an impromptu ride on Will out of her mind. Sure the motion of the train left little to the imagination, but for the first time since they had reunited she wasn't in the mood. She was focused on the task in hand, and annoyed at Will. And worried that if they were able to break the curse, he wouldn't want her anymore.

Will didn't know what he wanted. In the past he had a family, a wife children, and a whole friggin army. He had given all that up for what? A hot flame haired enchantress. She was hot. There was no denying that. And he was never able to control himself around her. And where did that get him? Cursed, and damned to spend his life scaring the shit out of any women he slept with. Of which there had been plenty. Woman threw themselves at him. He glanced over at Autumn, none of this was her fault. He invaded her village, and took her prisoner. He threw himself into the flames to save her. His wife cursed them. And now that there was a way to possibly break the curse, where would that leave him? Alone again? He went back to gazing blankly out of the window.

Finally the train arrived at the capital. They gathered up themselves, and their props. And made their way to the convention. Thankfully the closer they got to the venue, the more people in similar dress joined them. Wendy for one was starting to feel less self-conscious for a change. She still couldn't quite get fully used to being able to embrace her true elf self. Although having Kane at her side definitely helped her confidence. Even though he was human, he did make a very handsome elf.

Finders Keepers

Finally after ages spent queuing they made it inside the convention. Autumn couldn't help but feel overwhelmed by it all. It was like a giant indoor market. It was hot, and the scent of incense and warm, human bodies was almost too much to bear. It had been an age since she had lived in a time of no deodorant, but being in a convention soon took her back to those days. That said, there was so much energy in there to feed off of. And it was nothing to do a quick spell to mask the odour.

They all quickly split off into their teams. Apart from Brian, who suddenly felt abandoned and alone. He pushed all silly human thoughts out of his mind, and switched into cat mode. Then he was more than happy to stalk the stalls, looking for any possible sign of an enchanted blood stone.

It was Wendy and Kane who had the most amount of luck to start with. One particularly chatty stall holder knew rather a lot about magical, cursed stones. And even more about the lovers who were bound together by one. She was more than happy to share her knowledge of this curse with anyone who was willing to listen.

Standing up straight in her long, purple velvet robes she proudly stated, "I do happen to be something of an expert on a certain blood stone. It's such a beautiful, and tragic story. One of love, and hate all intertwined. Two lovers cursed out of jealousy. The brave, strong warrior prince, should have been allowed to enjoy all of the spoils of war. Including his captivating witch prisoner. But no, his evil wife killed them both. Burnt alive, can you imagine? And then locking them into a lifelong curse. Him to never find love, or happiness. Her to never find herself. All for as long as this stone is in existence. It's a tragic tale." She turned her gaze back to an impatient looking Wendy, and Kane.

Sensing Wendy's annoyance, it was all stuff they had heard, and read a million times Kane asked, "So what does the stone actually look like? Is there a description of it anywhere? Or an indication of who might have it now?"

"I don't have a clue what it looks like, no sorry. All I know is that it was said to be passed down through the wife's family. From her to her eldest daughter, and so on. A constant reminder of love, and betrayal. So by now it could be anywhere. That's if you believe the tale that is. I for one don't. I think it's a captivating story. But nothing more than that. I love the idea, two lovers, one a witch, the other a hot as hell warrior. Set out on a lifetime's mission to be reunited, but doomed forever to fail. All because of a magical stone. It certainly helps with the business. But is the stone real. In my opinion no."

With that Kane, and Wendy thanked the woman for her time. And walked away. Knowing that she wasn't that much of an expert. They knew the two doomed lovers. And despite the cursed stone, they had found each other. Although they doubted that part would ever make the history books. People seemed to love the idea of a doomed romance. Happy endings it seemed not so much.

Autumn and Will weren't having that much luck either. It didn't matter how much energy she had, she was coming up with nothing. She channelled Will's essence into herself, and even tried some blood magic. Dropping some of their blood onto a map of the venue, to see if it could seek the stone out. But nothing. The blood didn't even move. Which was odd in itself. They were both beginning to think the whole mission was pointless. A dead end. Maybe there was no stone after all.

Just as they were about to call it a day, Will stopped dead in his tracks. His eyes fell upon the face of a woman, which very much looked like his long dead first, and only wife. She had the same brown eyes, and long blonde hair. The very same heart shaped face. She was tall, and stood proud, standing out from the crowd. Around her neck, she wore on a leather cord a dark reddish brown heart shaped stone. It appeared to pulse as Will's eyes concentrated on it.

He didn't need to say a word to Autumn she felt it. Well the presence of it. It was protected, shielded from her by magic. And when she locked eyes on it, she saw it glow. The woman who had it around her neck seemed oblivious to the stones power. It was the curse that gave it power. Not the women wearing it. She was no witch, Autumn knew that. She was a descendant of Will's. She even moved like Will. Had all of his self-assuredness. His stance, and the way people looked at him. They looked at her in the same way. And so they should. She was related to a man that once, commanded, and conquered many Kingdoms.

That wasn't her concern now. She wasn't here to marvel at one of Will's living relations. It's not like they could have a family reunion. Or just walk up to her and say, "Oh by the way, this man's blood runs in your veins, and in that stone round your neck. And now we need it back." No she had to seize it using magic. Very strong, powerful magic. More than she could physically contain. After all if she couldn't use her magic to find the stone, she doubted her ability to obtain it with her skills, and inner strength.

Still she needed the stone. And this was possibly her one, and only chance to acquire it. There was plenty of energy in the air, and the city as a whole around her. All she needed to do was focus on that. And lock in on it. Once she had done that, she had to channel it into herself. Which was easier said than done, given the noise and commotion around her.

She held on to Will in order to find her focus. Then once she had as much power as she could harness running through her, she turned her attention to the necklace. She pictured it resting safely in the palm of her hand. No one would get it out of her grip. Not once she had her destiny in her hands.

All the lights flickered. Mobile phones buzzed. Windows vibrated. Then with an ear splitting high-pitched screech and a bang. It all went black. The necklace was in Autumn's hand. And she hit the floor. Will felt her fall. And after he registered what had happened scooped her up. And the necklace that was hanging loosely in the palm of her right hand. And fled from the venue.

It didn't take a miracle for the others to figure out what had happened. They to quickly fled the scene, as panic erupted around them. It took Autumn a few seconds whilst outside to regain consciousness. And a little longer again before she had the strength to put everything right. She had caused so much damage, that once she set it all straight. And had every pain of glass restored, and mobile device working, she passed out again.

Once the lights came back on, everyone was shocked, and stunned. And mostly relieved and confused by what had happened. The woman whom was wearing the necklace, took a moment to realise it was gone. She wasn't keen on it, but was sad it had gone. After all it had been in her family for years. She had wished it was a diamond, not some so called actual blood stone. But now it was gone, she felt a weight had been lifted from her. As the stone fed a little on her own life source to keep the curse alive.

PART FOUR

Recompense

And

Raptures

Homeward Bound

After everything that happened in the capital, they took the group decision not to stick around. Suddenly no one liked the idea of spending a night in a hotel. After all the fun and excitement they were all exhausted. And just wanted to get home. And get the stone to safety.

The journey home was much the same as the one there. In that they spent most of it in silence. Autumn was just starting to feel like herself again. And something about having the stone in close proximity to her made her feel, all hot and tingly. Will could feel it too. It was like it made his skin feel like a thousand tiny fairies were dancing all over it. It was annoying, and pleasurable all at the same time.

Finally there was nothing for it. Without saying a word Autumn stood up, and made her way to the toilet. Will soon followed her. The cubical was small, and didn't smell particularly pleasant. Will was still in possession of the blood stone. It was in his pocket. Without thinking he took it out, and went to put it around Autumn's neck. This in itself made her feel uncomfortable. She tried to back away from him, but found herself trapped between a sink, and a toilet. And pinned against the wall.

Will grabbed hold of her neck with one hand, and used the other to put the cord of the necklace around her neck. Looking into his eyes, it was like he was possessed. And for the first time since she knew him, Autumn was afraid. She was also unable to access her powers. How did he do this to her? Slowly he ran his hands down to her shoulders. Where still holding her tightly, he turned her round. She knew what was coming. There was nowhere to go. As he lifted up her dress, and forced her against the sink.

It was over almost as quickly as it began. He kept a firm grip on the cord around her neck, wrapping it around his hand. It cut into Autumn's neck, until she passed out. Even when she was unconscious he didn't stop. Not until he was ready to. When he was done, he let go of the cord, and left her slumped over the sink.

It took a few moments for her to regain consciousness. And then a few more to regain her composure. She was fuming, with her power slowing flowing back into her, she could have ripped the train apart. Instead she headed back to her seat. Will was already back with the others. Sat in silence. He was trying to figure out what had just happened.

Autumn didn't hide the marks left on her neck. She wanted the others to see what Will had done to her. She had taken the necklace off, and as she sat down she threw it at Wendy. Who after glancing from Will, to Autumn and back again, took the hint and stuffed it into her handbag. Brian was a little put out that Autumn didn't give the blood stone to him. But after closer observation of Autumn's wounds he decided, he didn't want the thing near him. It seemed to have a bad effect on who ever had it in their possession.

Destroy, or be Destroyed?

After a long day they were all relieved to be back at Brian's. It had been a busy, and productive day. They had achieved what they had set out to do. They now had the blood stone. At the start of the day, they didn't even know if it was real. Now it was sat in Wendy's bag. Sending out pulses of negative energy, and affecting the atmosphere in the room.

Autumn and Will still couldn't look at each other. They hadn't spoken since before the train journey. And the marks on her neck were getting worse. She still hadn't bothered to conceal or heal them. And Will didn't have the words to say, or explain how he felt. Or what had happened. The stone was trying its best to keep the two of them apart. And it looked like it was working.

When it all became too much, and being around Will, and Autumn was almost unbearable, Brian declared the stone must be destroyed. And no one was going to argue with him. Especially not the very unhappy couple. They were far too busy arguing with each other. The trouble was they didn't know how to destroy the stone.

After endless hours of looking online, all Wendy, Kane, and Brian met were dead ends. The only references they found were deeply shrouded by myths and legends. With no real truth in any of it. They were back to square one, except this time they had the stone, so they knew it was real.

Stan the Plan

After a busy Saturday shift, Wendy took off. She was going to meet some fellow elves with Kane. Who was much more excited about it than she was. As an elf there wasn't really anything about her own kind she didn't know. But to Kane, it was like a dream come true. As for Brian he was determined to catch Autumn alone, as he desperately needed to talk to her.

He asked her outright if she had given any thought to the stone, and the curse. And as she practically bit his head off about it, he took that as a yes. After she calmed down she did say she knew someone, a man, who might know a thing or two. He had helped her find the location of her own body. And was a self-proclaimed expert on the subject of her, and Will.

She didn't mention the part where they had a brief fling at the festival of magic. Or that she then burnt that body, and jumped into that of one of his friends. Infact she kept the details of how she knew him to a minimal amount of basic facts. She also didn't want Will to find out. She didn't think he would take too kindly to getting help, from one of her past conquests.

She also left it to Brian to track Stan down. She said it would be weird for her to get back into contact with him. The story she gave Brain was as follows. She met Stan in a library whilst doing some research. That bit was true. She was in the body of Cara, also true. Then she said they chatted over coffee, and arranged with some of his friends to go to the supposed place where the witch was burnt to death. She was a bit vague on the details of how she got her body back too. She told Brian that he was a bit of a fan boy, and meeting him again, as the witch he was obsessed with would be weird.

Not entirely sure he was convinced by Autumn's story, but not wanting to pry. He took out his phone and started looking for Stan. Needless to say it took a while, but after a few tweaks to the search he came across a social media page for him. And all it took then was to send him a message. Which was as follows,

Hey Stan,

I've have heard a lot about you from a friend of mine. It seems like we share a common love of a certain bewitched couple. I must say it's one of my favourite love stories, and hear that you are the total expert on the subject. Would love to chat to you about it some time.

Thanks Brian

It didn't take Stan long to reply,

Hi Brian,

I am always pleased to hear from people who share my love for this story. I for one have reason to believe it is more than just a myth. That there is some truth, hidden in this beautiful and tragic tale.

Kind Regards

Stan

Oh really, that's interesting. I would really like to believe that this story is true. Please tell me what you know, I'm all ears ☺

Brian

Well Brian,

All I can say is that I do have some experience, and I'm proud to say first hand, of this certain witch. If you would believe it? I am more than convinced that I witnesses with my own eyes, something magical. At the very place where the witch, and her lover were said to have been burnt.

Stan

Brian was starting to get frustrated now. He wanted to jump to the point. But also wanted to protect Autumn's identity. He didn't want it becoming common knowledge that she was real. It was one thing for the Parahumans to know. They were a secretive community, that lived amongst humans. But kept their powers, and true identities hidden. But for humans to know that such things existed. With the exception of Kane, that was not really allowed. As Wendy was well known for being a bit annoying, the Parahumans, elves mostly were just pleased she found someone.

Trying a change of tactic Brian moved the conversation on to the stone. Asking what if anything Stan knew about it. Was it in fact real? How important was it to the curse? All stuff he already knew. But his final question was, could it be destroyed? Stan was all too happy to talk about the stone.

Oh Brian,

I thought you would never ask. No one ever does. But I for one think the stone, is the pivotal part of the curse as you call it. Please allow me to explain more.

It all began the night before the two, ill-fated lovers met their untimely end. They were drugged by the man's evil wife. She had discovered that her husband was once again unfaithful to her. To add insult to injury it was with a witch! When he ordered his ale for the evening, she had her advisor drug it. The two of them were rendered unconscious.

Unable to fight back, she wanted them to be marked for what they did. More so her husband, she wanted him to have permanent reminders on him, of what he did. But also of what she, his wife could do to him. So she cut him, all over his arms and legs. Sure he had plenty of scars, but none from his wife. She was angry, and frenzied. She cut the witch too.

Then she collected some of their blood, and ordered that ropes be sent to her. She soaked the ropes in the blood. Then she had him bound in the ropes soaked in her blood, and her in his. Not wanting to stop there, she ordered the witch be burnt alive for what she did. She must have put a spell on her husband, it was the work of dark magic.

The witch was sent to the flames, and as her lover was coming to his senses, he saw her burning. Drugged still, bound in the ropes, and dazed he stumbled into the flames. The two of them burned together, and as their blood ran out of them, it joined together.

It is said that the wife saw the combining of the blood, and cursed it. And a stone was forged out of the blood, the flames, and the curse. The wife took the stone and left with it.

It is my personal belief that the stone, if it is indeed real can be destroyed. It must however be taken to the place where the curse was created. It should be destroyed in the same manner too, as when it was created. In blood, and fire. Only then will the curse, as you call it be lifted. Stan

Brian read the message to Autumn, and Will later that night. Will's reaction was that he never drank ale. He was a mead man. And that it would have taken more than a few drops, of something in his drink to knock him out. That aside if he was going to get himself burnt, he would have heroically thrown himself into the flames, to recuse Autumn. Not tumble into them, like some drunken fool.

Autumn on the other hand believed that there was some truth in Stan's words. He had been right about the place where they had met, both each other and their fate. Maybe he was right about the stone too. And as she knew where the place was now, it couldn't do any harm to go there and see.

Simple and hopefully affective

They still hadn't discussed life after the stone. None of them had. It was a real no go zone. And an area that wasn't worth the risk of getting into. All everyone knew was that Will was getting more aggressive towards Autumn, and she was becoming more withdrawn in herself. It was like the fire within her, that flowed out through her hair was being suffocated, and extinguished by the violence and turbulence of Will.

Autumn neglected to mention, in all the planning, and excitement that ensued one very important point about Phoenix Woods. It was now a housing development. She wasn't sure how much of it remained, or if the houses there were ever fully finished. She didn't know how keen they would be on going if they thought the possibility of committing arson was on the list.

Sure as she was now, she could easily reverse the damage. But what if after the curse was lifted she was human? She had to at least consider that possibility. Either way it was a risk she was willing to take. She couldn't carry on knowing that things with Will would get worse. And then that when she did eventually die, she would be reborn. And then have to carry on the same pointless search as before. Over, and over again.

It had to end, and if it meant burning down an entire forest. Houses and all, and then being human. It would all be worth it. She just hoped that they would all live to tell the tale. She did have a bit of a bad track record as far as fire was concerned. And liked the thought of having a normal life, without having the deaths of her friends, and loved ones hanging over her. That in her mind would be a thousand times worse than any curse.

There wasn't really a great deal of planning involved in this case. The plan in itself was very simple. Go to the woods, make a fire, throw some blood, Autumn's and Will's into the fire, along with the stone. Autumn would say a few magical incantations, and then they would all hope for the best. Whatever that was.

Back to the Start

It was Autumn's idea to go at night. She liked the idea of drawing on the power of the moon. And the animals of the night to brake the curse. Well that was her official word. In reality she thought they would have less chance of being seen at night. Even with a cloaking spell placed over them, she wasn't taking any chances, especially not where the stone was concerned.

They all piled into Will's car. It was big, black, and apparently the most comfortable. Although none of the others, aside from Will and Autumn felt comfortable sitting on the back seats. If Will and Autumn had been in the car, pre-discovering the blood stone, they daren't think what might have happened on those seats. As for the not so happy couple now, the anger, hate, and tension between them just added to the overall discomfort of the whole situation. And journey as a whole.

Autumn gave the directions, retracing the steps she took on her journey from the woods. It was one hell of a lot quicker going in a car, than it was on foot. And despite everyone insisting on using their phones to find the quickest route, Autumn assured them all, that her magic was far superior to that of modern technology. Besides she didn't want them to see what Phoenix Woods really was.

The big signs on the entrance kind of gave the game away. And Autumn mentally kicked herself. She could have hidden them with magic. Sometimes she wished she used a brain more. It was too late now though they all had an idea, at least as to what was to come.

The sight itself seemed deserted. It didn't look like to Autumn much more had been done since she had last been there. Which was a massive relief. The plan would have taken on a whole new, horrible twist if the houses were full of people. She did have a few flashes back to when she lived there before. When she was banished to the woods, and her people had a small settlement, that had been invaded by Will, and his men.

Wendy and Kane looked at the houses with envy. All apart from the one that looked like it had been destroyed by fire. They all seemed happy to ignore that one. Kane and Wendy would have loved to have a place like any one of those houses. Somewhere to call their own, where they could be together. And maybe one day raise a family. They weren't really thinking about Autumn and Will. They just wanted the whole thing to be over, so they could think about themselves and their own future together.

As for Brian, being a witch's cat wasn't as much fun as he thought it would be. When it was all over for him, he just wanted his independence back, so he could roam freely, and be his own man/cat again. He would be as loyal as he could be to Autumn, but in truth he missed Cara. And wanted her back, she was much more fun than fiery, loved up Autumn.

Fire, Blood, Sex, and Stone

Autumn decided the safest place to start the fire, was in the grass clearing. She hoped it would be far enough away from all the houses. She didn't fancy burning down the whole estate. She would only have to fix all the damage after. If she could, and besides she had other plans for the rest of the night. Provided everything worked, and the curse was lifted.

Wendy helped Autumn set up the fire, which only further exasperated Brian. As Autumn's witchy accomplice, and familiar, he should have been the one setting up the fire. Not the common old elf. Still he was optimistic that it would all go to plan, and he could get back to his life. One he decided without Autumn in it.

Will and Kane stood back, the girls seemed to know what they were doing. And Kane just wanted to make sure that Will stayed away from Autumn, and the fire. The way he was acting towards her, Kane couldn't be sure that he wouldn't throw her into the fire, along with the stone. Although part of him was a little beyond caring at that point.

The moon was high and full, and now directly above the fire. Without a second thought, Autumn tossed the stone into the fire. Nothing happened, accept that it rolled back out. Not a great start to the plan. She then had the idea to drop hers, and Will's blood onto it, and try again. Same thing happened. Her hair was tied up in a high ponytail, she untied it, as she suddenly had a brainwave. She dripped her blood onto it, and the Wendy handed the band to Kane, who passed it to Will. He added his blood to it, and threw it to Brian.

Brian was at this point tempted to throw the hairband onto the fire, without the stone. Being the better, bigger person, he handed it to Autumn. She wrapped the blood soaked band around the stone. And threw it back into the flames. Still nothing happened.

The tension in the group was now at critical point. Everyone was beyond fed up, and losing their patience. Nothing was working. In the end Brian picked up the stone, and out of annoyance more than anything else, launched it into the flames. It flickered a bit, and burned with a brighter more intense flame. They all held their breaths, hoping this was finally it. It wasn't, the stone flew out of the flames and landed on the grass. Which instantly caught fire.

Autumn put the fire out with a flick of her left hand. And picked up the stone it was still cold. Then she had a new idea. The stone was forged out of jealously. Maybe it needed that element to break the curse. And she was certain her plan would definitely install jealousy in at least one of the party. Will.

She pulled Brain to the side, and finally told him the truth about Stan. The whole Truth. He was also there when she was reunited with her body. Maybe he could be a key to unlocking the curse. Brian reached for his phone, and sent Stan a rather hurried message.

Hi Stan,

Please meet me in Phoenix Woods. I can't explain over message. But something is about to go down. And I think you would be insane to miss it

B xx

Straight away Stan messaged back,

Hi Brian

I'm on my way

Stan

Stan didn't even give it a second thought. The mention of Phoenix Woods was enough for him. Even if it was a hoax, or wind up he couldn't take the chance. He drove through the night as fast as he could in order to get there. He needed to know as much as he could about the witch, and her lover. He was a distance relative of Will's. The story had been passed down the family line, for generations. This was how he knew so much about them. And things that weren't in the textbooks, or online.

When he arrived on the scene, things were fractious. Wendy and Kane were looking at the houses. Brian had turned into a cat, and was hunting a mouse to kill time. Autumn and will were at opposite sides of the clearing. Stan couldn't believe what he was seeing. The sight of

Autumn and Will, just like they had walked straight of his imagination. She was the exact image of the red haired enigma that ran out of the house, the last time he was here.

Will was the first one to address Stan. "Can I help you? Are you lost? Would you like me to throw you into the fire?"

Brian quickly turned back into a human, and rushed over to Stan. It was the perfect moment to introduce them. "Will, meet Stan, he was here when, Cara aka Autumn found her original form. And new knew Cara very well by all accounts."

Stan's eyes lit up. "Wait so Cara, is Autumn? As in the witch from the story. That well we all know isn't an actual story. And I know this for many reasons. One of them being that myself and Will here are related."

Will was about to pick Stan up, and throw him into the fire. He got right up close to him, his voice boiling with rage. Jealous rage. "Let me get a few things straight here, whoever you think you fucked, it wasn't the real Autumn not really. Not her body anyway. If you touch that then you better hope it's right next to your grave. Because that's where you'll end up. And I'm sure as hell I'm not related to a dick like you!"

Autumn ran over to add to the atmosphere that was about to explode. She then called Kane, and Wendy over. One of them was in possession of the stone. Now all that needed to be decided was who was going to throw in the stone. Stan, or Will? Autumn didn't know about Stan's claim, that he was a descendant of Will's when she signalled that he should have the stone.

Kane stepped forward, and passed the stone, now wrapped in two blood soaked pieces of fabric ripped from Kane's t-shirt. One soaked in Will's blood, the other in Autumn's. He didn't need to be told twice what to do. But what he did instead, no one expected. He took Autumn's hand, she had no reason to be afraid, until he threw her into the flames.

Full of anger, and bound by the curse, and by love to Autumn Will threw himself into the fire. Then Stan threw in the stone. The screams inside the flames were horrifying. The pain, and agony, and stench of burning flesh was almost too much to take. And the heat, and light, from the flames was so extreme, no one could stand near to it, let alone look at it.

Stan was spot on with what he had done. The only part he had wrong, was the part where he was related to Will. The reason it worked, was that he was related to Will's wife, but not to Will himself. She went on to have children after Will was dead to her.

After the flames turned into a fireball, and imploded. Two figures stepped hand in hand out of the flames. They had once again been reborn, this time into mortals. They only had this life together, to live out together. And then that was it. Their story was all over.

Thankfully Brian had the forward thinking to bring spare clothes for Autumn, and Will. Any plan that involved burning, was sure to lead to some damages. It was just unfortunate that Kane didn't have a top to change into not that Wendy minded.

Deciding that his part in the story was more than fulfilled, Stan took off. He didn't want to face the wrath of Will. Mortal or not, he was still the same man he was all those years ago. Still had the same temper, and inclination to use it when needed. And Stan didn't see any reason to antagonise him further.

As for the others, Will told Kane to take them back in his car. And Kane was all too happy to oblige. The old Will would never have let him drive any of his cars. So Kane decided to take off before Will had a change of heart. Brian, said he was going to get back to hunting. He needed to spend some time with his inner cat. So Kane, and Wendy took full advantage of having Will's car all to themselves. And extra advantage of the back seats.

Still got it

Alone in the woods, back where they first met. Will took Autumn into his arms and carried her deep into the darkness. Finding a clearing far away from the empty houses, he carefully placed her down. Autumn was almost shocked by his gentleness. Maybe he really was a new man.

Just as she was getting used to the idea of a softer Will. One where he was on top of her, kissing her and running his fingers through her hair. Neither of them had bothered getting dressed, in the extra clothes Brian kindly provided. It was all skin on skin. Perfect pure, previously untouched skin. Which felt extra sensitive, and tingled with intense passion as they pressed up against each other.

Will was keen to explore all of Autumn, from the lips on her face, to her neck. Over all the curves of her body, and finally his lips landed between her legs. And his tongue tasted that part of her for the first time, all over again. She didn't have long to enjoy the experience. Before she could learn to handle all the feelings, and emotions that were rushing through her, he was kissing her again.

They spent the rest of the night all over, and in each other. No position or body part was left unexplored. Earlobes were nibbled, backs were very nearly torn apart. Hair was pulled, there was a good deal of Will grabbing Autumn round the neck, and he bent and twisted her until she thought her body would break. It really was access all areas. Nothing, and nowhere was out of bounds.

Night gave way to day, and as the sun poured down on them, they finally disengaged from each other. Hot, naked, and exhausted Will covered his eyes. The sun was blinding him. Autumn then had an idea, she hadn't tried her powers out. She didn't know how far this cure for the curse would go.

Clicking her fingers, she was thrilled when she was wearing sunglasses. Sensing Will's annoyance, she took them off and passed them to him. So it would seem that they still had it. Her magic, and his temper. As for where it would take them? They hadn't planned that far ahead.

The story continues in book 2 of the 'Curse of Love Chronicles'

Hunter's Moon

19457832R00076

Printed in Poland
by Amazon Fulfillment
Poland Sp. z o.o., Wrocław